Sword in the Snow

Matthew Harffy was born in Birmingham and has gone on to spend much of his life travelling, living in Spain and then Spain. He is the author of the Bernicia Chronicles and the forthcoming new series of books, as well as the standalone novels, *Wolf of Wessex* and *Dark Frontier*. He is also co-host of Rock, Paper, Swords! The Historical Action and Adventure Podcast.

Matthew lives in Wiltshire, with his wife, their two daughters and a slightly mad dog.

www.matthewharffy.com

Steven A. McKay was born in Scotland in 1977. He is the author of the Forest Lord, Alfred the Great, and Warrior Druid of Britain historical fiction series, as well as the standalone Roman slave novel, *Lucia*. He plays the guitar, listens to heavy metal, and lives just outside Glasgow with his wife, two children, and their wardog, Pippi.

www.stevenamckay.com

SWORDS IN THE SNOW

BY

MATTHEW HARFFY
&
STEVEN A. McKAY

Copyright © 2025
All rights reserved. No part of this book may be reproduced,
in whole or in part, without prior written permission
from the copyright holder.

CHAPTER ONE

ALL SAINTS' CHURCH, PONTEFRACT, DECEMBER, c. AD 1330

Father Reynardine le Page knelt and crossed himself, eyes closed, giving thanks to God for another day of good health and contentment. It was dark outside, but he'd been unable to sleep, a nervous jittering in his legs tormenting him until, at last, he'd had enough and decided to come into the church to pray. Candles were expensive, of course, so he'd only lit one, and it sat on the altar now, doing its best to beat back the gloom. The priest, a middle-aged, stout man of average height, imagined the flickering shadows as Satan's minions, stretching out their hideous fingers to steal his soul while the meagre light from the candle – and le Page's unshakeable faith – fought to keep them at bay.

He smiled, knowing the bishop would scold him for such flights of fancy, but the priest had always had a fertile imagination, and it gave him pleasure to picture little scenes playing out in his head. Sometimes he was the hero, other times he would imagine an apostle, or even Christ himself coming to his aid as the denizens of hell sought to drag All Saints' Church all the way from Pontefract to the Stygian depths below.

Le Page had made the mistake – once, only once! – of telling the sexton about his latest imaginings. The sexton, an older man, reported the tale to Bishop Wulstan on his next visit to All Saints' and

Le Page had found himself on the end of a dressing down. Apparently the bishop saw such fantasising as sacrilegious and forbade any more of it. The priest had meekly apologised and promised never to play out such Satanic vignettes in his head again but storytelling – even just to himself – was ingrained in his soul. Bishop Wulstan might think it wicked, but it made the long days, and even longer December nights, far more enjoyable when one could indulge in warming fantasies.

Didn't everyone indulge in those same imaginings? His eyes fell on the most valuable item within the church, worth more than all the gold and silver combined: the carved wooden statue called the Virgin of the Mountains. It was a pleasant enough relic to look upon, being about ten inches tall and depicting a seated Virgin Mary with the baby Jesus on her lap. Painted in vibrant, rich colours, and with the faces being particularly realistically carved, it was said to have been touched by the Apostle Andrew himself. Some claimed it could heal illness or injuries, and others ascribed even more outlandish stories to the little figurine, suggesting the Virgin had shed tears of blood during the great famine of 1316.

Father le Page was a deeply devout man, but he had to wonder if attributing wondrous miracles to such a nondescript wooden statue was any more fantastic than imagining Christ standing beside him, helping to fight back the darkness that lurked in the corners.

It was late, approaching midnight, and the silence was so deep that it only added to the atmosphere, giving the priest's lively imagination plenty to work with. The church was situated on its own plot of land a short distance away from the surrounding roads, themselves deserted at this time of night, so it really did feel like Father le Page was all alone in the world. He prayed silently, barely even registering how cold it was in the stone building with its lofty roof, hard floor, and single flickering candle.

Suddenly there was a noise behind him and, for a moment, he ignored it, thinking it simply the timber doors of the west entrance contracting after the day's heat. Then he remembered there had been no heat that day – there had been a frost and fog that never lifted, so why would the wood be creaking in such a manner?

The priest's blood ran cold as an even louder thump came then, and the candle on the altar flickered as though a gust of wind had blown it.

Had the devil's brood come to tempt him? Or, more likely, to savage him with claws and teeth as sharp as knives? Images of towering demons filled his mind, their lumbering forms accompanied by bright hellfire and—

"There's someone here. You said the place would be deserted, you bloody oaf!"

"Shut your mouth. I said it was *usually* deserted at this time."

Father le Page felt frozen to the spot, kneeling on the cold floor, unable to turn and look at whoever had just forced their way into the church, damaging the lock in the process from the sounds of it.

A third voice, that of a younger man, piped up. "It's alright, look. It's just one man, and he's a priest. No threat."

"Deal with him then," the first voice rumbled, as deep as hell itself, suggesting a lumbering bear of a man.

"And then find what we came for," said the second voice. "I'd like to be out of here before Christmas Day!"

Father le Page heard footsteps coming towards him and anger flared within him. Anger, and outrage that his prayers had been disturbed by three ruffians, there for no good purpose. He rose stiffly to his feet, ignoring the ache in his knees, and spun to face the person coming along the aisle towards him.

The priest saw a young man, jaw set firmly as though steeling himself for the task he'd been given. The dim light showed few details of the youth's face and, when le Page tried to see the other intruders he could make out only dark shapes. He squinted at the foremost of those shadowy figures, striding purposefully along the west aisle.

Was it truly a demon? From the sheer bulk of the intruder it was hard to think of him as anything other than supernatural, for he was absolutely enormous in both height and build.

Something struck him in the face and he reeled back, more surprised than hurt. He steadied himself and turned back to the youth, frowning as he saw the young man's raised fists and bared teeth, and Father le Page understood what had happened.

"You hit me," the priest said, feeling desperately sorry for himself and rubbing his aching jaw, tears filling his eyes. He had never been struck in his life! His mind raced, trying to make sense of what was going on, but, as his attacker came forward again Father le Page felt a sudden surge of rage fill him. These men were common thieves!

It was just like the stories he made up in his head, he thought, when the powers of evil sought to overcome those of good.

To his own astonishment, the priest threw himself on the young man, hands clawing at the intruder's pale throat, squeezing as he cried out for God and His saints to give him strength. Somehow in his frantic thrashing he landed a painful blow, for his opponent cried out and pushed away from him, hands clutching between his legs.

"Can you do nothing right?"

The priest, wide-eyed and still enraged, turned, and all his courage evaporated like frost on a sunny morning. The huge intruder was lumbering towards him, face as black as a thunderstorm, and before le Page could think to escape, he was slapped in the side of the head.

The blow felt like it had been delivered by a warhammer rather than a human palm, and the priest was lifted off his feet, falling sideways to sprawl on the floor, a terrible ringing in his ear. Before he could move, the giant kicked him in the stomach and he gasped, feeling all the air blasted from his lungs. Desperately, he tried to breathe, unable to move as that hateful, monstrous boot cannoned into his face and darkness swept over him.

CHAPTER TWO

"God's bones, Tuck, why is it so dark?"

The man in the grey cassock looked up at his huge friend and chuckled, shaking his tonsured head good-naturedly. "It's December, John. What do you expect?"

"I don't expect it to be night in the middle of the day!"

John Little was almost seven feet tall, but he was walking through town bent over like an old man, huddling into his cloak and rubbing his numb hands against the chill. He – like his companion Robert Stafford, better known as Friar Tuck – had once been a member of the infamous outlaw gang led by Robin Hood. In those days they were used to living outdoors, sleeping in tents or caves as the wind whipped snow and icy rain around them. Now, in his mid-thirties and employed by the Sheriff as a bailiff of sorts, John spent most of his nights tucked up either in his own cosy house in Wakefield, or at a lodging house if he was travelling.

"Pah, it's hardly night," Tuck retorted. "You've just grown soft."

"Soft!" John straightened to his full height, glaring down at the friar so fiercely that passersby hurried away, glancing over their shoulder at the angry, bearded giant in their midst.

"Aye, soft," Tuck repeated, laughing again as he continued to walk through the drab streets of Pontefract. "Not so long ago you'd have been thanking God for such a fine, dry day."

John shook his head and followed his burly friend. Maybe Tuck was right, he had been as tough as oak when he was a wolf's head – they all were, the friar included – but, well, it was bloody dark and cold, and all the bailiff wanted was to sit by a fire and enjoy a few ales.

Little John was not like other bailiffs who generally lived in and oversaw a particular village. Instead, Sir Henry de Faucumberg, the Sheriff of Nottingham and Yorkshire, employed the former outlaw as more of a roving lawman, sending him to deal with those men and women who'd proved too troublesome for the local bailiffs or guards to deal with. Often, his reputation and his huge physical presence were enough to bring transgressors into line, and they would pay their fines or capitulate without trouble when John visited them. If they did choose to resist, well, John had earned a reputation as a skilled warrior with good reason. Although his friends and family knew him as a warm, affable, and loyal companion, those who stood against him cursed his brutality and the feared quarterstaff that had broken so many enemy bones.

Friar Tuck was almost as dangerous in a fight, having been trained as a wrestler in his younger days, and he knew how to wield a sword or staff just as skilfully as his giant friend. He was, ostensibly a man of peace, of course – a churchman, not a lawman. He'd accompanied John to Pontefract simply because he liked the place, particularly the baker's shop near All Saints' Church on the northern side of the town.

"I'm not even sure you can call this 'dry'," John grumbled, holding out his hand to show Tuck the mist that coated it. "Even with these mittens on, my fingers feel like they're about to fall off."

"Oh stop complaining," Tuck grinned, spotting the baker's shop just ahead of them. "Look, we're here. One of those nice warm pies will soon sort your frozen fingers."

"Food. Is that all you think about?"

"Well, don't you buy anything then. Wait here and I'll get some for myself."

John cursed the friar and followed him towards the shop, mouth already watering as the scents of wood-smoke, roasted meat, and freshly baked pastries filtered out into the frosty street. There was an alehouse just past the church too, he remembered, and, since he'd already completed the job the sheriff had given him, he planned to head there with Tuck and their hot savouries before making their way home to Wakefield.

"Tuck!" The shout rang out, loud in the still winter air, and John, recognising a distinct note of alarm in it, spun around, staff held defensively before him. At his side, Tuck was in a similar posture, ready for whatever an enemy might throw at them, but the cry came again and the bailiff realised it had come from someone standing at the entrance to All Saints' Church.

"Is that Bishop Wulstan?"

John squinted as the clergyman stepped out from the doorway and the pale December day lit his features. "Aye, it is," the bailiff nodded. "Something's upset him too."

"Come over, Tuck," the bishop called almost frantically. "And you too, John."

With a last, longing look at the baker's, both men sighed and walked across to the church. It was not a particularly large building, but it was impressive nonetheless, having been built quite recently.

Bishop Wulstan Barnsford had met John and Tuck before, when they'd investigated a strange, and ultimately murderous, religious sect. The bishop had led the trial against the leader of the cult, Lady Alice de Staynton, whose punishment was excommunication and banishment. He was a competent, clever man who did not seem the type to be easily upset, so John was surprised to note how pale the bishop's complexion was. He was wringing his hands as the former outlaws strode across the road and, as they reached him, he let out a long sigh that conveyed great relief, as if he was glad to meet someone who could take the weight from his shoulders.

"What's happened, your grace?" Tuck asked, reading the signs as John had done.

In reply, Bishop Wulstan turned, beckoning for them to follow as he went into All Saints'.

The pair did as they were bidden and walked inside, both tugging their collars up for it was even colder in the church than it was outside, their breath steaming in the frigid, incense-tinged air as they walked.

"In the name of God!" Tuck cried, hurrying ahead as they saw a priest lying on his side on the floor, eyes open but clearly in great pain and distress. "Stand back," the friar commanded and the two men who were kneeling beside the priest hastily moved aside to let him through. They might have no idea who the burly newcomer was, but his tone brooked no argument.

John looked on, bemused, as Tuck, a man of learning who'd often acted as healer or surgeon for Robin Hood's outlaw gang, tended to the injured priest who had, at least, been covered with a blanket.

"What happened here?" the friar asked.

"Thieves," said the fallen clergyman, grunting in pain as Tuck checked him for broken bones. "They came in the night. I tried to stop them, but there was a giant with them and he—" His eyes fell on Little John and he visibly shrank into himself, terror written across his bruised face.

"As big as him?" Tuck asked incredulously.

The priest, who must have thought his attacker had returned to finish what he'd started, slowly realised that John was a different person. He nodded, sobbing softly. "At least as big," he said. "Maybe even bigger."

John frowned and shared a glance with the bishop. There weren't many people in England as tall as Little John, and the thought of such a person going around stealing from churches and attacking priests was truly disturbing.

"It's worrying indeed," said Wulstan. "The baker across the road was working late and came to check when he heard shouting. He found Father le Page lying there unconscious." The bishop gestured with his arm towards the altar. "The thieves have cleared the place out. A proper inventory will have to be taken."

An older man came into the church then.

"Ah, sexton," the bishop greeted him.

"Your grace!" the old man responded, wide-eyed at the unexpected scene. "What's been going on?"

"Thieves. I'll explain it all later. For now, would you take a look around and see what's been stolen?"

"Of course, your grace." The sexton made the sign of the cross and wrung his cloth cap in his hands, nodding and murmuring prayers to himself as he moved around the aisles, taking mental note of the precious items that had been taken by the intruders.

"Has anyone gone after the men who did this?" John asked, turning away from the sexton.

Yes," Wulstan confirmed. "The baker raised the hue and cry."

"In the middle of the night?" John muttered wryly. "He'll have been popular."

"Indeed. I believe six men went after the thieves. God willing, they'll be back soon with the miscreants in tow."

There was a thump at the door, and a broad-shouldered young man stumbled inside, blood streaming from a wound on his forehead.

"Speak of the devil!" Bishop Wulstan cried. "That must be one of our fellows. Help me, bailiff."

John moved to prop up the injured man, assisting the bishop in guiding him across to a stone bench set against one of the walls.

"Where's the rest of your men?" John demanded. "Six of you, I was told, went after the thieves."

"True enough," came the reply, and the bailiff noticed the man's mouth was also bloody, and missing the front teeth, impeding his speech. "Six of us went after the bastards. Only two of us made it back. The other lad has a broken leg. I left him about a mile back, in the care of a taverner."

"Two survivors!" Bishop Wulstan exploded. "But there were only three thieves."

"Aye, and they fought like demons," the injured man replied sourly. "One of them was like a bloody giant. Bigger than you," he added, looking up at John. "Maybe."

"Let me see your head," Tuck ordered, shouldering his way past John and gently touching the cut on the newcomer's skin. "Nasty, but not too deep," he pronounced. "We'll bandage it up and you'll be fine after a mug or two of ale. Nothing I can do about your teeth though, I'm afraid."

"What kind of thieves are these men?" the bishop asked, taking John aside so Tuck could tend to his patient. "Outnumbered two to one, yet they still managed to win, and escape, murdering four of the town militia in the process?"

John shook his head. "It's a bad business right enough," he growled. "Only scum steal from a church."

They stood in thoughtful silence, brooding over the savage raid that had left so many men dead or wounded, and All Saints' bereft of its gold and silver treasures.

"It's gone!"

John and Bishop Wulstan jerked around at the anguished shriek, looking towards the altar. The sexton stood there, mouth hanging open like a dead fish.

"It's gone, your grace," he cried again. "The Virgin of the Mountains. They've stolen the relic!"

"What? God's blood, no!" Bishop Wulstan ran down the aisle, holding up his long cassock as he went, seemingly too shocked to care how undignified his run was.

"What relic?" John asked as Tuck, who'd finished bandaging the wounded militia-man, came to stand beside him.

"Virgin of the Mountains," said the friar, repeating the name the sexton had used. "It's just a carved wooden statue, to look at anyway."

"Exactly," said the bishop. He'd inspected the altar and found the sexton's claim to be correct. "No normal thief would steal such a thing."

"A relic dealer then?" Tuck asked. "Someone hired by a client to steal this item for a personal collection?" It was not exactly a rare crime – there was even a name for it: *furta sacra,* or 'holy theft'.

"It must be," the bishop groaned, dropping down to sit beside the man with the bandaged head. John wasn't sure which of the two looked most sickly.

"If the relic ends up in the hands of a collector we'll never see it again," said Tuck in disgust. "Things like gold chalices or crosses are usually sold on by thieves – they can be traced, bought back, the men who took them arrested even, if their trail is not well hidden. But if the Virgin of the Mountains is being taken to a collector it might never resurface."

"And by the time Sheriff de Faucumberg sends competent men here to investigate, the thieves will be long gone," Bishop Wulstan said, head dropping into his hands. "Christ help us, that relic is priceless! The apostle, Andrew, touched it! It's performed miracles! Pontefract has never had anything like it before and, in fact, we have two parents bringing a sick child here within the coming days to be healed, God willing, by the relic."

"A child?" Tuck asked.

"Yes," the bishop replied fretfully. "A little poor girl – the daughter of one of my own servants, actually. She is, well, she's dying. No one knows what's wrong with her, exactly, and no one has been able to help her. A peasant's diet can't have helped. The Lady of the Mountains was the family's last, desperate hope." Suddenly his head snapped up and he was on his feet, eyes blazing with righteous fury. "You two have been sent here by God," he said.

"No, I came here to—"

"Never mind that." The bishop broke in before John could finish, a manic grin on his usually cultured face. "It's no mere coincidence that you and Tuck just happened to be standing outside All Saints' just after the relic was stolen. God sent you here!"

"Why?"

"Why? To go after the thieves of course! To bring back the relic and save that girl!"

"Oh, not this again," John murmured, turning to look at Tuck in dismay. "Not another Christmas where we're chasing around the countryside after dangerous lunatics."

"Praise Jesus, thank you!" Bishop Wulstan cried, raising his hands and staring up at the roof beams, tears in his eyes.

"Will you go after them?" the militia man with the bandage on his head asked. "I wouldn't recommend it. They'll kill you, just like they killed the lads that went with me."

"Of course they'll go!" the bishop snapped. "Won't you, John? Tuck? You thrive on danger!"

"Oh, aye," John groaned sarcastically. "We just love chasing after murdering giants in the middle of winter!"

"Good, it's settled then! You best be off immediately."

"But what about the baker?" Tuck asked plaintively as John ushered him out of the church. "What about the pies to warm our cold fingers?"

"They rode to the north!" called the man with the bandaged head as they stepped out into the frozen afternoon. "May God help you, lads. You'll need it!"

CHAPTER THREE

Henry Tanner reined in the chestnut palfrey beside the swaying gibbet. A crow had been digging its dark beak into the putrefying flesh of the corpse that hung within the frame. The dead man's eyes, always the first morsels to be eaten by the carrion birds, were long gone. At Tanner's approach, the crow croaked in annoyance and flapped away from the creaking scaffold. It landed in the bare branches of a beech tree alongside several other of its black brethren. The tree and the crows were stark against the slate sky.

A gust of chill wind rattled the tree, tearing some of the few remaining leaves from the boughs. The body in the rusted iron frame of the gibbet spun slowly, as if turning to greet Tanner. He looked away, pulling his woollen cloak tight around his neck. Despite the deerskin gloves he wore, his fingers were stiff from the cold.

Far-off, the peal of bells echoed across the brittle, early morning landscape. The faithful were being called to Prime.

If he thought God would have listened to him, Tanner might have prayed that it would not snow before they reached their destination. Sniffing, he hawked and spat. His spittle flecked the skein of ice that rimed the deep puddles made by the carts and wagons on the road to York. Tanner didn't pray. He had long since turned his back on God, as the Almighty had abandoned him.

Another blast of wind made Tanner squint. There was snow in the air for sure. Some way behind them, he could make out the figure of Richard Blount beside the road near a stand of spindly alders. Tanner had thought the young man had dismounted to take a piss, but Dick hadn't climbed into the saddle again and he was now crouching beside the saw-backed nag that Wake had given him for the journey.

"Go and see what trouble that fool has got himself into now," Tanner snarled.

He knew he would be better off riding back to investigate for himself, but he was tired and hungry, as well as cold. Tanner was unsure he could trust himself not to beat the young fool, if he found he was wasting their time, and that would only delay them further.

It had been a long night. They would not be warm and rested until they passed through the gates of the city. Even so, Tanner welcomed a moment's respite from the constant yammering of their young companion. He was tempted to leave him behind, but such things had a habit of coming back and biting him in the rump. Dick knew too much about his affairs and those of their master to allow him to be captured by the Sheriff's men.

The other rider, a huge, bearded brute of a man, grunted and wheeled his horse around. Tanner watched as his companion kicked his heels into the flanks of the tall, broad-chested stallion. The animal was as large as a destrier, but this was a horse bred for the plough, rather than war. Anything smaller would be unable to carry Grimbald de Pendok for any distance. A massive man, with the strength and temper of a baited bear, Tanner had seen Grimbald snap a man's arm with his bare hands, all the while grinning, his yellow teeth, flashing from within the dark thatch of his beard. It was one of the few times he had seen the man smile. Tanner liked Grimbald even less than he cared for Richard Blount. But at least the giant only spoke when absolutely needed. Tanner had barely heard the man utter more than a dozen words in the six months he'd known him. In fact, he wondered whether Grimbald knew any more words. He had certainly seen no indication that Grimbald had more than the intellect of the bear he so closely resembled.

Tanner watched for a while as Grimbald's horse lumbered back along the muddy path. Scouring the frigid distance, he saw no tell-tale signs of pursuit. No flocks of birds disturbed by riders. No evidence that any more of the militia, or the Sheriff's men, had followed them.

Grimbald had almost reached Dick now and Tanner turned his attention to the northeast. Dick was frightened of Grimbald and would stop whatever foolishness had detained him quickly enough. Grimbald possessed even less patience than Tanner when it came to young Richard Blount.

The pall of smoke on the far-off horizon, a brown smudge on the grey, showed Tanner the location of York. Early morning mist was thick over the River Ouse, but that would soon be blown away by the bitter wind that was picking up.

The bells of the city's many churches had fallen silent now. Tanner shivered and again hoped it would not snow before they were safely inside Wake's warm tavern. Fleetingly, he thought of the townsfolk flocking into the cool interiors of the churches. Katerina would be with the worshippers in Skipton. He could picture his wife kneeling with the rest of the clods in their blind hope for miracles, pleading with the Almighty to help them with their ills, aid their harvests, or to see that they got a good price for their wares at market.

Some of them might pray for the Lord to heal their children.

Tanner had no time for such nonsense. Absently, he patted his saddlebags, feeling the bulk of the object inside. Most people believed, despite seeing nothing to back up their faith in this world of pain, sickness, greed and cruelty. More fools them. Luckily for him, some such believers had deep pockets.

The gibbet creaked in the wind and he glanced up at the ruin that had once been a man. He wondered what he had been hanged for. Then, with a start, Tanner knew the answer. This criminal had been caught stealing from Nicholas de Langton, the Mayor of York. Tanner sighed, his breath steaming. He knew well enough the man's crime. He should. It had been his doing that had seen him captured by the city guards.

The corpse's long hair, as luxuriant as any woman's, was plain to see now that the gibbet had rotated with the wind. Few men wore their hair so long. Once the hue of burnished gold, it was streaked with silver now. Tanner peered up at the face. Despite the bloated and blackened features, there could be no doubt. This was Johannes de Thexton.

They had been friends once, John de Thexton and he. Long ago it seemed now. Tanner recalled how frequently John had brushed his hair, much to the amusement of the other men serving with them in Robert de Clifford's retinue. Even on the morning before the horror of Bannockburn, John had run his carved antler comb though his locks until his hair shone. Tanner had liked him back then. He was loud and boisterous, and full of bravado. Thexton had even saved his life in that terrible battle against the Scots, blocking a mace-blow meant for Tanner after he had been knocked down into the churned mud.

For a time after the rout, they had travelled together, falling in with other soldiers fleeing southward. Soon though, they had each gone their own way. From time to time over the years they would see each other. It was always good to catch up on old times over an ale or, more likely, several.

Tanner had put in a good word for Thexton when he had come begging William Wake for work. Times were hard and Wake had been reticent to take on another old soldier, but Tanner had vouched for John. He owed him his life after all. It was the least he could do.

If John had imagined his past with Tanner meant he could steal from William Wake with impunity, he was more of a fool than Grimbald.

The first time Tanner had seen him pocket coins from the tavern table when a fight broke out, he had confronted John in the courtyard after the drunk merchants had been cast into the street.

"John," he said, catching Thexton by the arm, "if you steal from Wake, you steal from me."

Wake had promised Tanner a cut of the profits from the gambling at The Black Swan. All Tanner needed to do was see that nobody took more than their agreed share. When Thexton had come looking for work, the job seemed made for him. Out of his own share, Tanner paid John to keep an eye on things in the tavern while he was busy elsewhere in the city. His soldier friend was a solid, tough man, able to handle himself. His presence alone kept all but the rowdiest patrons in check.

"Who's stealing, Hal?" Thexton said. He tried to shrug off Tanner's grip, but Henry grasped him tightly, pulling him around to face him.

"How long have you been lining your pouch?" he asked. He had noticed the weekly takings had been down of late, but there was always some excuse or other. Tanner cursed himself, recalling how Raynald, the old taverner, had tried to warn him about Thexton. He'd dismissed the old man's loosely veiled comments, but now knew Ray had been right.

"It's just a few pennies," said Thexton, his face growing scarlet. Digging into the pouch on his belt, he pulled out a handful of coins.

"Keep the money," Tanner said, his voice cold. "But it stops now. You understand me? We go back a long way, you and I, John."

Johannes scowled.

"You owe me," he said, his tone sour.

"Aye," said Tanner with a sigh. "There's no need to remind me. That's why we are still talking. Anyone else would have a knife in their guts already." He fixed Thexton with a hard stare. "You won't get a second chance. You hear me? If I catch you again, or if Wake gets wind of this, you're a dead man."

Tanner stared at the rotting corpse. It was hard to imagine that until a couple of weeks prior, the horrific thing had been Johannes de Thexton, filled with vitality and humour. Tanner shook his head and again spat into the icy mud. Had Thexton believed his warning to be nothing more than wind?

It had been a month later when Raynald had told Tanner that Thexton was at it again. Tanner had asked the taverner to watch him, at the same time apologising for not listening sooner. The old man bore him no grudge, nor did he appear to take any pleasure from snitching on Thexton.

Henry didn't bother confronting Johannes a second time. He had given him more than a fair warning. He watched him closely for a few days and, when he was certain Thexton was indeed stealing, he knew exactly what to do about it.

Just the week before, on Martinmas, William Wake had summoned Tanner to the small room above the tavern where he conducted the most secretive of his business transactions.

And the bloodiest.

An unplanned audience with Wake was seldom a good thing. When Tanner saw Grimbald was there too, silent and ominous, he had known he was in trouble. There was no doubt in Tanner's mind to whom the huge man owed his allegiance. Or what Grimbald was there for.

William Wake was a slim, wiry man, his greying hair cut short, his beard neatly trimmed. The clothes he wore were plain, yet expensive. Charcoal-grey doublet, blue hose and polished black shoes. He sat in a large, comfortable chair made of dark-stained oak. There was little to mark him as extraordinary. He could have been a clerk, a scrivener, or a tradesman.

Except for his eyes.

Tanner had seldom seen William Wake blink, and when he had made the mistake of looking into the man's dark eyes, he had felt as if he was staring into deep, cold pits. Wake nodded at a chair that placed Tanner with his back to Grimbald. Trying not to show his nervousness, Tanner sat.

"You happy, Hal?" Wake asked, sipping from a cup of the expensive Rhenish wine he had Raynald serve only to him and his most trusted associates. Tanner was not much of a wine drinker, preferring ale, but he noted with alarm Wake did not offer him a cup.

"Happy?" he asked warily. He forced himself not to glance over his shoulder at Grimbald.

"Working with me," Wake said, unblinking.

"Of course." Tanner sensed the danger in the room. He wasn't sure what he had done to displease Wake, but he'd attended many such meetings and occupied the position Grimbald stood in often enough to know how this was likely to end. "Have I done something wrong, Master Wake?"

Wake ignored the question. With a show of relaxed calm, he leaned back in his chair. The polished oak creaked. From the tavern floor below came the sound of singing and a gust of laughter.

"Call me William, please," he said. "I consider you a business partner, you know? And am I not good to my partners?"

Tanner chose his next words very carefully.

"You've always been fair to me, William."

"I have, haven't I?" Wake placed his cup gently on the table. "Then why are you," his voice rose into a sudden rage-filled shout, "swiving me up the arse?"

Tanner swallowed. He knew better than to reply. He remained silent, allowing Wake's anger to subside.

Wake took a long breath, brushing imaginary dust from his doublet. Slowly, he reached for his cup and took a sip.

"Avarice," he said at last. "Greed. Cupidity. *Radix malorum*. The root of sin, so the clergy say. I don't give a fig about sin, but even we must act within certain constraints. We need never want for anything, you and I. There is no need to be greedy."

Tanner saw where this was going now.

"I sought your permission for the house-breaching work, and I paid you your dues as agreed."

"So you did, so you did." Wake sat back and stared at him for a time. "You're a good lad. I know it, but you have taken the burglaries too far. They have to stop now. Grim," he snapped his fingers, "fetch a cup for Hal here."

Grimbald grunted and Tanner heard the giant moving about the room. A part of his mind wondered whether the request for a cup was some pre-arranged code for something a lot less pleasant than a drink of wine. He resisted the urge to look behind him.

"We have almost free rein in the city," Wake continued. "All I have to do is to keep certain palms greased. And we have to be discreet. You know that. You are no fool."

Grimbald reached past Tanner and placed an empty cup on the table before him. Tanner let his pent-up breath out. His tension began to ebb away. Wake nodded at the jug of wine.

"Help yourself."

Tanner poured while Wake went on.

"Do you know what discreet means?"

"I know what it means," Tanner replied. And now he knew what he had done, too. "I'm sorry."

"So am I," said Wake, a glimmer of a smile on his face. "You are daring, for sure, but to steal from the Mayor himself! Did you spare any thought about how to sell the thing you took such a risk to pilfer?"

"It is made of solid gold," Tanner said. The wine was sweet and rich. Tanner took a small sip. It would not do to relax too much. "I had thought to melt it down."

"Tell me you have done no such thing," Wake said.

"I have not."

"Good. That livery collar is worth far more to us than its weight in gold. It is very hard for those in the city watch whom we count as friends to continue to look the other way, when Nicholas de Langton is screaming at them, denouncing the Watch as incompetent and demanding justice."

"You are right," Tanner said. "It was foolish of me."

"Of course I am right. You will cease any activities I have not ordered directly, and you will see that de Langton is reunited with his precious collar and badge of office. Now, finish your wine and go. You have work to do."

Tanner drained his cup and rose. Grimbald glowered at him from the shadows. He looked disappointed. No doubt he would have preferred to have been commanded to kill Tanner. The man's lust for blood was chilling.

"Hal," Wake said, halting him as he reached for the door, "this is your only warning. I like you, and you have done well up to now. But I can find other partners."

Grimbald had sneered at Tanner as he left the dingy room.

Thexton had provided Tanner with the perfect solution to his problem. It took no effort to hide the livery collar in Johannes's room. One of the friendlier members of the city watch was all too happy to accept information from a butcher who was in Tanner's debt saying that he had witnessed Thexton climbing from the Mayor's window on the night of the burglary. A surprisingly small bribe ensured that few questions were asked of the butcher, and that Johannes de Thexton, a known ruffian and a previously convicted thief, was slain while being arrested. Nicholas de Langton was reunited with his undamaged golden collar, the captain of the Watch received his thanks, and another bribe.

In that single night, Tanner had been rid of his problematic erstwhile friend, and Wake was content that the focus of the Mayor would once again shift away from crime in the city.

The sound of hoof beats on the road behind him cut through Tanner's memories. It sounded to him as if only one horse was approaching. Sure enough, Grimbald was riding back towards him, his bulky horse sending up splatters of mud and ice as it plodded along.

"What's the trouble?" Tanner snapped.

"Lost a shoe," replied Grimbald.

Dick was leading his horse along the road towards them. His expression was pinched, dejected.

"Is the nag lame?" shouted Tanner.

"She's got a nasty limp, she has," Dick replied.

Tanner drew in a long breath. How he wished Wake hadn't made him travel with these two. Even as he thought it, he knew it was unfair. He might have ridden faster without them, but if the Sheriff's men had caught up with him alone, he would be dead now, or a prisoner on his way to join Johannes de Thexton in a local gibbet.

"My horse is tired and cannot take two riders," Tanner said after weighing up their options. "Grim's horse could easily carry you both. You can lead that bag of bones."

Grimbald shook his head.

"The boy is not riding with me."

Without waiting for a reply, he kicked his horse into a lumbering trot and headed in the direction of York. Tanner watched him go and sighed again.

"You heard him," Tanner said, "we cannot tarry here. You'll have to ride, shoe or no shoe."

"The poor mare will be lame in no time," Dick said, his tone miserable and whining.

"Just get that horse to the city, and then to the knackers. It's more bone than anything."

Dick patted the animal's neck and whispered something in its ear.

"But what if she can't carry me all the way?" he said, pulling himself up into the saddle.

"Then you'll have to run to keep up," replied Tanner, pulling his palfrey's head towards the city. With a last glance at what was left of Johannes de Thexton, he spurred his mount on, not waiting for Dick's reply.

CHAPTER FOUR

Dick's horse managed to carry him all the way to York. The animal was hobbling and lame, but it had plodded on until they had reached Micklegate Barre, the southernmost gate into the city. Snow had begun to fall from the thick, low cloud that enveloped the winter sky. Tanner was pleased to see there weren't as many people crowded about the city gate as there would have been on a market day, or if the weather was more clement.

"Get down and lead the poor thing from here," Tanner barked. Since leaving the gibbet, he had ridden close to the young man, in case the mare had not proven strong enough. That had meant he had needed to listen to Dick prattle about their encounter with the Sheriff's men during the night.

The boy was tough enough, in the way of street urchins. He'd been in his share of scuffles and brawls. He'd even witnessed a few more serious beatings and a couple of murders while in the employ of William Wake. But he had never served under one of the king's lords; had not donned armour and taken up shield and weapon to stand, trembling in the great heaving press of men as thousands of screaming, murderous Scotsmen charged towards you with nothing more in their mind than to stab their wicked blades into your flesh.

To Dick Blount, the skirmish with the six guardsmen who had ridden after them from Pontefract was a glorious battle. He had been nervous before the fighting started. Who wouldn't be? Tanner had fought in battles where the earth turned to a quagmire of blood, shit and piss. He had killed more men than he remembered, and he was still terrified before a fight. Only a fool, or a madman, would feel no fear before waging war. That was at least something Dick had over Grimbald. The boy might chatter like an excited child, but at least he had the common sense to be scared of men wielding swords. Grimbald had shown no emotion beyond a mute, savage pleasure at the killing.

Tanner had not expected to be followed so soon, but they had heard the bell ringing the alarm in the darkness and, some time later, the clatter of their pursuers' horses. He had prepared the ambush as well as he was able with the limited time available, sweeping out of the night as the riders slowed to negotiate a swollen ford. With the element of surprise, they had killed four of the men in moments. They should have killed all of them he knew, but Dick had attacked too soon, warning the last two of the trap they were riding into. They had wheeled their horses around, colliding in their panic and both falling into the road. One had screamed out in agony, and had needed his companion to help him back into the saddle. But before Tanner, Grim or Dick could close with them, they had galloped back in the direction they had come. Tanner didn't think the men had got a good look at any of them, but Grimbald was huge, and even in the black of the winter's night, such a giant would be remembered.

"Poor creature," Dick said, slipping from the saddle. He patted the horse on its skinny neck.

"You carried me well, old girl." Then, turning up to look at Tanner, who remained in the saddle: "I still can't believe I got one of the bastards."

"Shut your mouth," hissed Tanner, glancing at the watchmen standing by the imposing structure of the city gate. There was not such a throng before the entrance as there sometimes was, but there were still several people close by. There was only so far bribes and favours would go. "Say nothing more. You hear me? If I have to listen to any more of your shit, I'll turn you in to the Sheriff's men myself. And for one who killed some of their own, they won't be picky if you're alive or dead."

Dick swallowed, his cheeks red. Mercifully, he kept quiet. With a growl, Tanner pulled his palfrey's head towards the stone gatehouse that protected the archway into the city. They fell into line behind a waggon laden with barrels. A skinny, dirty girl sat on the back of the vehicle, her filthy bare feet kicking aimlessly as she silently eyed Tanner and Blount. Something about her guileless gaze reminded Tanner of his daughter, May. Clenching his jaw tight, he scanned the people ahead of them. They shuffled forward as the merchants, farmers, tradesmen and other assorted travellers funnelled in through the gate past the bored eyes of the City Watch guards.

Tanner sighed with relief as he saw what he had been searching for.

"Let me do the talking," he whispered. Dick glowered up at him, looking more like a chastised child than the tough man he believed himself to be. Thankfully, he said nothing.

The snow was falling thick and fast now, settling on the ramparts of the wall and on the edges of the road where grass and weeds grew. The ground before the gates was a black, cloying mud. Nobody had joined the queue of people waiting to enter the city behind them and Tanner silently cursed Dick for slowing them down. He had hoped to avoid the usual morning rush.

Grimbald, sitting tall on his huge horse, reached the gate and rode into the city. He had not waited for them. Tanner's horse was much faster than the huge stallion Grimbald rode, but Tanner had chosen to remain with Dick, whose nag had limped slowly over the last mile or two. Still, it was probably for the best that they were not seen entering the city together.

The girl on the waggon stared at Tanner. Beneath the grime, she was pretty, with large, thoughtful eyes and an expressive mouth. He felt the urge to smile at her, but couldn't manage to summon any friendliness into his features. After a time, she looked away from the scowling, scarred man who rode behind her father's waggon.

At last the waggon passed beneath the Micklegate arch. Tanner nudged his mount forward and reined in beside the watchman to the right who stood beside a smoking brazier. The gate was in shadow and the thickset man had his arms wrapped about his chest, his hands stuffed beneath his arms. His nose was red from the cold and he sniffed as he looked up with a morose, vacant expression. On seeing Tanner, his demeanour changed. He stood up straight, casting a furtive glance at his companions.

"You're out early, Hal," he said.

Tanner gave the slightest shake of his head. He knew this watchman. He was easy enough to bribe, but Tanner found him too familiar by far.

"No," Tanner said, his voice low and even, "I am not. Neither is he." He nodded towards the young man leading the limping mare.

For a moment, the round-faced guard looked bemused. Tanner leaned down from the saddle and pressed a shilling he had prepared into the watchman's hand.

"Right," said the man, giving a knowing wink. "I never saw you."

Tanner held on to the man's hand.

"Good. If I hear otherwise," he said, tightening his grip so the guard could not pull away, "I'll remember seeing *you*." The threat in his voice was clear. The guard licked his lips, nodding nervously. Tanner held his gaze for a second more, then released his hold on the man and rode on.

When they were out of earshot of the gate, Dick could remain silent no longer.

"One day, men will look at me the way that guard looked at you." He was breathless with excitement, as if he had witnessed an alchemist's magic, instead of a simple bribe.

"Nobody will look at you any way at all if I have to listen to any more of your wittering," Tanner said, his tone savage. "Now, take that sorry beast to the butcher's yard. See that you get a fair price, then come straight back to The Black Swan. And remember, that horse is Wake's, so the price for it is his. If I hear you've spent any of it, or stopped at a stew, you'll regret it."

CHAPTER FIVE

Tanner made his way over the Ouse Bridge, paying the toll without comment. Rarely at ease, he enjoyed the welcome feeling of being surrounded by the city. Ever since leaving Pontefract, he had felt as if more men would come galloping over the horizon at any moment. York had been his home for several years now, he knew its streets and alleyways, and had friends, or at least men and women who were indebted to him or William Wake, on every corner.

Turning down the narrow lane that led to his destination, Tanner ducked to avoid the overhanging buildings that loomed above him, almost completely shutting out the light. It would have been easier to walk and lead the horse, but his boots were quite clean and the street's cobbles were thick with deep mud and all manner of offal and refuse. The animal's hooves churned up the mess, and the stench made him cough. Tanner loved the city, but he had to admit, by and large the countryside smelt better.

He allowed the palfrey to pick its own way down the lane and turn into the Black Swan's yard. The animal knew the way well enough and it nickered a greeting to the other horses standing beneath the lean-to that served as a shelter for the beasts. Grimbald's huge horse was already tied there. A young boy, pale and grubby in the cold, was brushing the animal.

The yard was not much better than the lane outside and Tanner was careful where he put his feet as he dismounted. The snow was still coming down, and the shingled roof of the tavern and the planks that made up the roof of the shelter that acted as a stable were already white.

He handed his reins to the boy.

"See that you brush, water and feed him well."

The shivering lad nodded, but would not meet Tanner's eye. His left cheek was red. Tanner reached out and the boy flinched.

"Hold still," he said. The boy tensed and sniffed, but did not move. Taking the lad's chin in his hand, Tanner turned his head. The bruise on his cheek was fresh. It appeared to be swelling even as Tanner examined him. He did not need to ask the lad what had happened. It was not the first time Grimbald had lashed out at him. For some reason he loathed the child, though Tanner had never heard or seen the boy do anything to warrant the abuse he received.

"See to Grim's horse first," Tanner said, removing the saddlebags and slinging them over his shoulder. "When you are done with mine, come into the warm and I'll see you get something to eat. And don't worry about him. He won't touch you while I'm around."

The boy sniffed again and wiped his nose on the sleeve of his tunic. Without a word, he led the palfrey under the lean-to.

Tanner made his way across the yard and pushed open the door. It was quiet inside, devoid of the drinkers and gamblers who would fill the smoky room during the evening. A fire burnt bright on the hearth, popping and crackling, but only adding a meagre glow to the scant light filtering through the translucent hide stretched over the small windows. The room smelt of spilt ale, old piss, sweat, boiled cabbage and damp wool. In short, it smelt like any other ale-house. To Tanner, it smelt like home.

Off to the side of the room, Raynald was chopping vegetables that Tanner knew would be swept into the perpetual pottage that always simmered in the large iron cauldron hanging beside the fire. The taverner nodded in welcome, but said nothing. He was a man of few words, but Tanner detected a tension in him and caught his glance towards the rear of the room.

There, at the furthest table sat William Wake. Before him, a flagon of ale in his meaty hands, sat Grimbald.

"Good morrow to you," Tanner said to Raynald, who grunted and kept chopping at the turnip on the scored wooden board.

Tugging off his gloves, Tanner went to the fire, stretching his fingers out to the heat. He would have welcomed a moment to collect his thoughts before seeing Wake. Some time to allow the warmth back into his bones after the long ride. But Wake was not a man to be kept waiting.

"Grim says you ran into some trouble," William Wake said.

Tanner stared at the flames for a couple of heartbeats before replying.

"Grimbald would do well not to open his mouth so much," he said, "lest he gets a boot in it."

Grimbald growled and made as if to rise. Wake waved a hand for him to stay seated.

"Now, now, Hal," he said. "Grim doesn't say much. When he does, I tend to listen."

"I prefer it when he's just silent and stupid. It makes his stupidity easier to bear."

Grimbald growled again.

"You would do well not to pick a fight with me," he rumbled.

"And you would do well not to hit Adam whenever you see him." Tanner's anger bubbled up and he spun away from the hearth to face Grimbald. His hand dropped to the hilt of the sword he wore. "He's just a child."

"He is just the stable boy," said Grimbald. "And I barely touched him. If he doesn't want to be hit, he should be quicker to do my bidding. Anyone would think he was your bastard, the way you carry on. Or perhaps you are sweet on young boys."

Wake looked from Tanner to Grimbald. After a moment's consideration, he placed a hand on Grimbald's arm.

"Take your ale upstairs," he said. "I'll have Raynald bring up some food for you."

Grimbald glowered at Tanner, his eyes burning with hatred. Pushing himself up from the table, he snatched up the flagon and a cup and strode out of the room, ducking his head under a thick beam as he thumped up the stairs and out of sight.

Wake sighed and beckoned for Tanner to sit where Grimbald had been seated.

"Raynald," he said, "some warmed ale for Hal. And perhaps some cheese. Is there any bread?"

"Aye," replied Raynald, "some ham and sausage too."

"Good, good," said Wake. "I am sure Hal is hungry. And don't forget to take some up to Grim. You wouldn't want to end up with your ears boxed like Adam." Wake grinned at the idea. Raynald scowled, but made no comment. Tanner wondered whether he was imagining Wake or Grimbald as he took his cleaver and began ferociously hacking at a leg of ham.

Tanner slung the saddlebags from his shoulder and onto the table. Wake looked at the leather bags but did not move to open them.

"That it?" he said, at last.

"We got what we were looking for," Tanner replied "Perhaps best we don't open it here though." He glanced at the door.

"Raynald isn't looking, or listening." Wake raised his voice. "Isn't that right, Ray?"

The taverner looked up from where he was placing slices of ham and sausage onto a trencher of bread.

"Huh?"

"See?" said Wake with a grin. "You really shouldn't goad Grim, you know. One day he'll turn around and gut you."

"He can try," Tanner said. "He seems to prefer hitting little boys though. And farm labourers."

Wake's eyes narrowed, picking up on Tanner's tone.

"Trouble?"

"Plenty, but nothing we couldn't handle. Grim beat a man senseless yesterday for a harmless jest. Drew undue attention."

"You went through Leeds, like we discussed?"

Tanner nodded. They had decided to take a less direct route to Pontefract as an extra precaution against being remembered by travellers on the road.

Wake pursed his lips.

"Perhaps no bad thing to call attention then. Should throw anyone on your trail off the scent."

Tanner scowled.

"Perhaps," he conceded. "But the man's a liability."

"Just don't forget who you both work for," said Wake.

"I thought we were partners."

Wake smiled without humour.

"Don't test my patience, Hal. There is too much riding on this. Talking of boys, where's Dick?"

"Taking that old nag you gave him to the butcher. It could barely carry him all the way back."

Wake frowned.

"That mare had another year or two left in her."

"If you had fed her, she might well have lived that long, but she wasn't going to be any use for riding or pulling a cart. All she's good for now is meat and tallow."

Wake didn't look happy with the fate of the horse, but he moved on quickly, as was his way.

"Grim said the boy fought well."

Tanner grunted. Raynald came over carrying the bread, cold meat and cheese in one hand, a mug of ale in the other. Tanner pushed the saddlebags out of the way, making room on the table.

"Dick didn't piss himself or run away," he said. "That's something."

"How bad was it?"

With a cloth wrapped around his hand, Raynald pulled a poker from the fire. He brought it over and dipped it into Tanner's ale. It sizzled and steamed. Tanner thanked him and sipped the warm drink. He waited until the taverner had trudged up the stairs with a trencher for Grimbald before replying.

"Bad enough," he said. "Four men dead. Two got away."

Wake sucked his teeth and cursed under his breath.

"Do you think they recognised you? Could you be tracked back here?"

Tanner shrugged, chewing a piece of the hard, crumbly cheese. It was salty and strong-flavoured.

"Grimbald's a hard man to hide, even in the dark. But there was nobody on our trail when we reached the city walls."

"We'll have to hope the Sheriff doesn't have any men of worth who could follow you."

"Still, might be best to lie low for a time. You said the buyer was from France?"

"I've arranged to meet with his agent in Ravenser Odd, a week from now." Wake scratched his neck, just beneath the line of his beard. "Perhaps you are right. It wouldn't do any harm to have you and the others take the piece there. No point in dawdling here if there is any chance you might have been followed."

Tanner's heart sank. He had hoped to spend the next few days in the city. Since Johannes had gone, there was nobody he trusted to watch the tavern and see that he received his rightful share of the gambling. But Wake was right. What the French benefactor had promised them was more than he would make in months from his cut from the tavern.

"Very well," he said, "but I need some sleep first." He couldn't face the thought of riding out into the freezing countryside straight away. "I suppose you want me to take Dick and Grim with me."

"Of course," said Wake, with a twisted smile. "You make such a good team."

Tanner let out a long breath and took a deep draught of the warm ale. He closed his eyes, taking a moment to enjoy the drink and the hush of the tavern. His mind was already turning to his bed and what he would do once he had slept for a while. The days were short at this time of year. By the time he had rested, it would be dark and he would have to stay for the night.

That suited Tanner. He was planning on visiting the strumpets down Grope Lane. There was no place for romance in his life, but he was still a man. Besides, the bawd at the stew he oversaw had been slow with her payments. If he didn't check up on her regularly, he knew she would hold back what was coming to him.

CHAPTER SIX

As it turned out, Little John decided they should visit the baker after all. The baker had been the one to discover Father le Page, so it made sense to question him. He'd not been able to tell them much, since he'd turned up at All Saints' after the attackers had escaped – on purpose, no doubt, although neither John nor Tuck could blame him for avoiding danger. Besides, he'd been most helpful in furnishing them with two steaming hot meat pies and some cold ones for the road. The pair had returned to their horses at the nearby stables with full bellies, determined to bring the criminals to justice.

They rode out of town, heading northwards as the injured member of the hue-and-cry had directed.

"Did you get a description of the fugitives when you were bandaging that fellow's head?" John asked, eyes continually scanning the land as they made their way along the road. "How was he anyway? Will he be alright?"

Tuck shrugged, guiding his mount around a patch of ice. "He should be, if he takes care of himself and cleans the wound regularly. As for a description, aye, I asked, but I didn't get much from him. Three men, two normal sized, another about as big as you or even bigger. One of them was young."

"It's not the most detailed description," John agreed. "But there's not many folk as tall as me in the north of England – that will at least give us something to go on."

"As big as you, eh?" Tuck shook his head and blew out a breath, fingering the cudgel that he habitually wore tucked inside his cassock. "I'm not looking forward to coming up against him."

"Leave that bastard to me," John rumbled confidently. "We'll see how hard he is when he's up against someone his own size that isn't a man of the faith. Speaking of faith, d'you think the relic can really heal that little girl?"

Tuck shrugged expansively. "Maybe. It's happened before."

"Perhaps, if the bishop believes the girl's food has something to do with her condition, he should be paying the girl's mother more."

"No doubt," the friar agreed. "But lets give him some credit for trying to help them now, eh? It's not every peasant gets the chance to be in contact with a relic like the Virgin of the Mountains."

As they rode, they passed other travellers and asked them all if they'd seen the escaped criminals. None had and, by mid-afternoon John was beginning to get irritated. It was already growing dark and the mist was thickening into a damp, icy fog that soaked clothing and almost seeped into one's very bones.

"This is getting us nowhere," the bailiff muttered, still scanning the horizon, and the road ahead, for some sign of their quarry. "Are we even going in the right direction? You'd think someone would have seen the men we hunt. What if we're going the wrong way? We'll never find them!"

"Let's stop for a while," Tuck suggested. "As you say, there's no point in going on if we're heading in the wrong direction. Look, there's a village up ahead, let's see if there's an alehouse. Perhaps someone there will be able to help us."

John nodded. "Fair enough, my beard's got frost in it, and it'll be good to thaw out a little. We're not going to get much farther today anyway. No moon to light the road, and if this fog gets any thicker we could end up going in circles."

As it turned out, the village they rode into was named Micklefield, and Little John was somewhat familiar with the place, having passed through more than once while on the sheriff's business. Geese hissed at them as they passed, but they ignored the birds, always on the lookout for more dangerous foes.

"There's the alehouse," John said, leading Tuck directly to a small building that looked like it might not hold more than a handful of people comfortably. "If it's not busy we can stay the night here, I think, so don't worry about having to find a place to pitch the tent."

"I don't mind sleeping in a tent," the friar replied, one eyebrow raised hopefully. "I'm more interested in what kind of food they serve at this alehouse."

"Ha!" John let out a bark of laughter, teeth flashing within his grizzled beard. "The same terrible food you get in any village alehouse up and down the length of England, Tuck! There'll be a choice of pottage, and pottage."

The burly friar nodded and patted his belly which let out a rumble as though in response. "Just as well I like pottage then, isn't it?"

"You like anything, Tuck, you fat ba—"

"I like punching big hairy oafs in the mouth," the friar broke in, waving his clenched fist at the bailiff. "So watch what you're saying."

"Charming," John grinned, sliding somewhat clumsily from his horse and stretching out his back and neck. "God, I hope they do have some food and ale, fresh and ready to serve. I'm not getting any younger."

"Aye, riding does take a toll more than it used to," Tuck agreed, dismounting with even less grace than his giant friend. "I'm more than a decade older than you, remember. But our aches and pains will soon be forgotten."

There was a stable beside the alehouse although it was extremely crude. Tuck eyed it doubtfully, but John led his mount inside and began making the horse comfortable for the night, removing saddle, bridle and other tack before brushing the animal down.

"Hurry up," he urged the friar. "It's good enough for a night. There's no stablehands, but there's food and water for the animals, and a roof, of sorts, to keep the frost off."

Tuck looked up at the rapidly darkening sky and muttered something about snow being likely, but he guided his palfrey into the stable and got to work. Soon both horses were safe, secure and quite content to be left alone.

As they were working, an old man with a straggly white beard walked past, stopping to gape in at them, wide-eyed, as though he'd never seen strangers in Micklefield. Before bailiff or friar could greet the man he hurried away, casting surreptitious glances back at them as he went.

Sharing an amused glance with Tuck, Little John stepped out from the stable and led the way into the alehouse. There was a single room with a low fire burning in the hearth and, as the newcomers bent low to pass through the front door without cracking their heads, a woman appeared from a back room.

She looked at them, openly sizing them up, then recognition flared in her eyes as she noticed John's prodigious height and gestured him forwards.

"Well met, bailiff," she said in a business-like tone. "You'll be wanting warmed ale, eh? Food?"

"Ale, food, and a place beside the fire there to spend the night, if that's agreeable to you, lady?"

"Agreeable enough," she said, walking past them to place another log in the fire. "You leave horses in the stables?"

"We did."

She nodded, working at the fire with the poker until the room was merrily lit and then, without another word, she disappeared through to the back room again.

John and Tuck sat on stools at a table that was rather too low for them but, when the alewife returned carrying mugs of ale and two bowls of steaming pottage any criticisms they might have harboured quickly disappeared.

"That'll be a shilling and six pence for the food, your horses' food, and your lodging," the woman said, sticking out a small palm which John immediately filled with coins. She looked at it, counting in her head, and then smiled for she'd been paid half a shilling more than requested. "If you want more ale or pottage just shout," she told them, and bustled off once more.

After second helpings of food, and several more ales, they took their blankets from their packs and settled down for the night on the floor. Although far from the comfiest bed either man was used to nowadays, the day's ride had tired them out and soon both were snoring contentedly.

* * *

In England, an outlaw – a wolf's head – could be killed by anyone. On top of that, the sheriff's men were forever on the hunt for those men and women who'd been classed as outside the law. It was an incredibly dangerous life, when one might find an arrow in their back or a sword in their belly at any moment. As a result, Little John's senses had become attuned to things that seemed out of the ordinary: an unusual smell on the breeze; a glance from a forester that lingered just a little too long; startled birds taking flight in the woods; whispered voices in the dead of night.

"Tuck!" The giant bailiff rolled to his knees, grabbing the quarterstaff that lay on the floor of the alehouse beside him. "Wake up," he hissed again, reaching out to shove his friend gently but firmly.

"What?" The friar came awake, a dazed look on his round face, but he too grasped his staff and rose to his feet, watching John quizzically.

The bailiff lifted a finger to his lips and nodded towards the door. "There's someone out there," he whispered into the friar's ear. "Sneaking about."

Tuck nodded and there came a low voice through the door, confirming John's claim.

"What d'you want to do?" Tuck murmured, eyes fixed on the door which was bolted shut but would not withstand even a single kick from a strong man. "It could be the men who raided All Saints'."

John frowned at the prospect. It seemed unlikely – how would the fugitives even know they were hunting them, much less know they'd stopped here for the night? Still, he could hear at least three voices outside and it seemed only logical to assume that whoever they belonged to had come to the alehouse specifically for John and Tuck. And it was highly unlikely that the visitors wished to give them a friendly welcome to the village in the middle of the night.

"Wait," he said softly, pressing himself against the wall. "See what they do."

Tuck nodded and took up a position on the other side of the door, face grim in the low light from the hearth which had almost burned itself out.

John strained to hear what the men outside were saying, the hands that grasped his enormous staff growing slick with sweat so he had to wipe them dry on his cloak. He did not feel particularly frightened – he'd fought in many battles as an outlaw, a soldier, and a bailiff. Still, Tuck's suggestion that it was the three thieves outside added an extra layer of danger to what was happening. Was there a giant as big as John himself

– bigger! – stalking the alehouse, prepared to kill those who'd been sent to bring them to justice?

Tuck jerked his head towards the door but John had already heard the footsteps approaching. If it was the thieves from Pontefract they were not exactly stealthy, and the bailiff braced himself, the blood thundering in his ears as he threw a feral, lupine grin at Tuck who returned it with glee.

The door shuddered and the iron latch gave way instantly, which surprised the man who'd kicked it as he stumbled inside, completely off balance and swearing loudly. The butt of John's quarterstaff slammed into his forehead and he collapsed in a sprawling, limp heap, unmoving and utterly silent.

"Hey!" Another man shouted at the doorway, but he jumped back as Tuck came out, expertly using his staff to keep the would-be attacker at bay. "You've killed him, you bloody lunatics!"

"We'll kill you too, if you don't throw down your weapon and tell us what you want," Tuck snarled, all trace of his usual devout demeanour gone. "Do it! Now!"

John came to stand beside his friend and noticed a third figure lurking further back, almost invisible in the shadowy street. "You," the bailiff shouted, walking forward and breaking into a run for just long enough to reach out a great, muscular arm and haul back the hooded cloak of the white-bearded old man who'd been staring at them in the stables earlier.

"That's not them!" the old man shouted, looking past John at the fellow who stood before Tuck, unarmed now having dropped his knife at the friar's command.

"What? Who the hell are they then?"

"I don't know," returned the white-beard. "I never got a good look at them before. I thought it was them!"

"You're seeing them now, in the middle of the night, in the dark, and *now* you can see it's not them, you stupid old bastard?"

"What are you two fools babbling about?" John demanded, giving the old man a shake, although not too hard for he feared snapping the elderly frame in two. "Who are we not?"

"We were attacked yesterday by travellers passing through the village," the old man replied plaintively. "One of the attackers was a big, huge, ugly oaf."

"I can see why you thought that was John," Tuck noted with a dry chuckle.

"So you thought you'd sneak up on us as we slept in the alehouse and what? Kill us?" John released the old man with a disgusted shove. "You and your friends move with all the grace of an angry boar. You made so much noise it woke us up, and now, well..." He turned and looked at the open doorway and the man he'd struck with his staff. "I don't think he's doing too well."

"Can I see to him?"

Tuck nodded and the man who'd relinquished his knife hurried past him, bending to examine the unmoving villager.

From within the alehouse came the sound of a door being unbolted and the alewife appeared, a massive skinning knife in her hand.

"By the bollocks of Saint Jerome," she cursed, causing Tuck to bless himself and murmur a prayer for her soul. "What's going on here?"

"These idiots mistook us for someone else," John said. "But I think everything is straightened out now. Well, apart from him. Can you help him, Tuck?"

It was clear the danger had passed and the old man tried to disappear into the darkness, but John grabbed his cloak again and guided him towards the alehouse. "You and your friend can come in and tell us all about these men who attacked you," he said, just as the unconscious man on the floor rolled onto his side and vomited, much to the alewife's fury.

The woman hurried away into the rear section of the building, coming back soon after with a wooden bucket and a rag, thrusting it at the whitebeard. "Get that puke cleaned off my floor, Charles, or you're barred!"

The old man seemed to wither even more under her terrifying glare and he meekly accepted the bucket, getting slowly, stiffly, down on his knees and, squinting at the sight and smell, did a terrible job of cleaning the mess.

When the injured man had been seen to and laid down on the floor to recuperate, the alewife brought drinks for the others and, once paid, went away back to her bed with a disdainful last glance at them all.

"What happened with these men who attacked you then?" Tuck asked, no longer a battle-hardened warrior, but a jovial friar once again.

Charles, still looking a tad green from cleaning the vomit, nodded to the other man who had by now retrieved the knife he'd discarded outside and tucked it safely back into its sheath. "Martin can tell you more than me," the white-beard said. "It was his brother that got knocked about."

"There's not much to tell," Martin sighed, a rueful look on his weather-beaten face. "We'd been working on a roof all morning, repairing the thatch, and stopped for a rest. The three travellers appeared along the western road, and my brother made a jest about how big one of them was." He took a long swallow of his ale and then held out his palms. "I mean, it was a harmless jest."

Charles piped up again, rheumy eyes glittering with amusement. "He said the big fellow must have fallen asleep in a pile of manure when he was a babe, that's how he'd grown so much."

John grunted having heard variations on the joke many times over the years. It might have been funny the first time but now? "I'm not surprised your brother got a slap," he growled.

"Aye, well, it was just a silly jest. The giant got down from his horse and punched my brother so hard he came right out his shoes! Then he told us all to fuck off and rode on his way, the two men with him not even glancing back to see if we were following them."

"Men used to dealing out violence, and unafraid of the consequences," Tuck murmured. "Certainly sounds like the ones we're after, John."

"It does, and that means we're on the right track." He turned back to Martin and Charles. "Did you hear them say where they were coming from?

Any clue that might help us find them? They robbed All Saints' in Pontefract last night, and hurt the priest there even more than they did your brother. Killed some of the militia men who chased after them too."

The old man crossed himself and muttered about things being better when he was a lad, while Martin merely shrugged.

"I doubt they came from any of the villages around here. Men like that would stick out like a sore thumb. Everyone would mark them."

"They must have come from a larger town, or even a city," John nodded, agreeing with the villager's deduction.

"Leeds," Tuck suggested. "That's the nearest big settlement, ten miles or so to the west, and even a giant wouldn't attract too much attention, what with all the weird and wonderful folks that live there."

"That makes sense," said John, satisfied that they now had a firm destination to ride towards. "Leeds has a few wealthy criminals. I'll wager the relic they stole is destined for some gang leader's personal collection."

"What time is it?" Tuck asked, getting up and opening the door to look out. The previous day's fog had lifted and the stars glittered merrily. He pulled his cassock up around his neck and came back to the fire. "It's the middle of the bloody night," he noted. "You three had best get home, while we try to get a couple more hours sleep."

"Sleep? After all that excitement?" John's laughter filled the small alehouse, bringing an angry rebuke from the alewife in the rear of the building. "I'll never get back to sleep after that," the bailiff reiterated in a quieter voice.

The villagers left with more apologies for their rash, foolish actions, helping their bruised friend along the benighted street to their homes. Within half an hour Tuck and John had jammed the alehouse door securely shut with a bench and were snoring by the hearth like hogs, oblivious to the alewife's shouted complaints.

CHAPTER SEVEN

The clear sky of the previous night had unfortunately given way to an icy drizzle as John and Friar Tuck said their farewells to the alewife who almost cracked a smile when the bailiff paid her far more than a fair price for the broken door to be repaired. The horses were in good fettle and seemed to be as eager as the men to get back on the road and run some warmth into their bones.

Hood up, John spat out a hard oat from the porridge they'd broken their fast on and muttered darkly about the weather.

"I know," Tuck agreed. "Even snow would be preferable to this insidious rain. May the good Lord put an end to it soon."

"At least Leeds isn't too far. We should be there in a couple of hours."

Tuck nodded and rearranged his cloak over his legs to try and keep them dry. "Into Leeds by early morning, find this giant and his mates, back to Pontefract with the relic by late afternoon?"

"Ha! Maybe God can arrange all that after he stops the rain."

They rode on for another half a mile or so and then the drizzle did ease up and the sun almost broke through the clouds, lifting the temperature just enough that it didn't feel like frostbite might set in.

"What's the story with this relic anyway?" the bailiff asked, opening his pack and helping himself to a piece of salted beef. "One of the apostles' bollocks or something is it?"

Tuck shook his head with a look of mock outrage. "You know fine well it's a statuette," the friar said. "A carved wooden depiction of the Virgin Mary and child Christ. Have you never heard of the Virgin of the Mountains?"

John shrugged. "Maybe. I don't think so. Feels like every church in England has some piece of the true cross, or one of Peter's fingers, or the spear of Longinus."

"I think you're exaggerating," the friar scolded. "Although it's true there are a lot of relics scattered about the country. Some of them might be fake, but many seem to be genuine, and some have great miracles ascribed to them."

"What makes this Virgin of the Mountains so special then?"

"You heard the bishop. It was said to have been touched by one of Jesus's Apostles, Andrew. It's cured the sick, healed injuries, and inspired countless Christians to devote themselves more fully to living good lives, helping others and so on."

John grunted. "I suppose that's good," he conceded. "Regardless of whether Andrew really did touch the thing. Have you ever seen it?"

"I have! Not in All Saints', I think it's only recently been taken there. Certainly it wasn't there when I last visited. But the way Bishop Wulstan described it, I've come to realise I came across it many years ago, when I was acting as a guard for the church. It was taken from Lewes Priory to a place somewhere on the east coast. I forget where exactly, but I was tasked with protecting the relic."

John nodded. He'd heard many tales of Tuck's adventures when bishops and other powerful churchmen had employed the former wrestler as a guard; they were always entertaining and a reminder that the friar was more than a simple man of God.

"I remember it quite clearly," Tuck went on. "The face of little Christ in particular was…" He smiled and shook his head. "It had a certain power to it, despite being a simple carving of wood."

John murmured agreement. "Sometimes the simple things are more moving than those made of gold and silver that cost a fortune."

"Indeed. You'll understand why the Lady of the Mountains is so revered, and wanted back by Bishop Wulstan so badly, once we retrieve it from those thieves. It is truly holy, John."

"Well, God willing, it'll be in our hands soon and it heals that little girl. Look." He jerked his chin upwards and Tuck smiled.

"Leeds," said the friar. "We're here. And well before midday. D'you think there's a baker here too?"

John merely snorted in reply, and they were soon at the town gates. Although Leeds was classed as a large settlement when compared to somewhere like Micklefield, it was not as sprawling as a city like London or York. Still, there was a queue of waggons waiting to enter the town, and John rode past them with Tuck following close behind.

"Who are you?" a guard challenged them as they reached the gates, but the man's face split into a broad grin as he recognised the enormous bailiff. Having been a celebrated outlaw, a champion of the people, Little John was a popular figure all over

Northern England. "What brings you here?" the guard asked as the riders dismounted.

"We're looking for some thieves," the bailiff told him. "Tuck and I have been tasked with finding the men who robbed All Saints' Church in Pontefract. They nearly killed the priest, and then murdered four of the town militia who chased after them. You haven't seen three dangerous looking thugs, have you, friend? One of them is supposedly as big as me."

"Bigger," Tuck added helpfully, smiling as John shot him a disdainful glance.

The guard's eyes widened. "No, I've not seen anyone like that coming through. Sounds like they'd be hard to miss too." He paused, face screwed up, and then he raised a finger, nodding vigorously. "Wait, I think I did see three men like that a couple of days ago, although only from a distance, for I'd just come back from taking a piss and they'd already passed through the gates. They were riding south, I remember that, and looked to be in a hurry."

"Shit," John cursed.

"Maybe one of the other guards spoke with them," the man suggested. "Feel free to ask around. Failing that, try at the inns and alehouses. Good luck." He nodded respectfully to them and stood aside to let them pass through, walking with their horses.

As it turned out, none of the other guards on duty had seen the fugitives and so John took Tuck to speak with the proprietors of the local drinking establishments. It was a similar story in those too, with no-one having seen any giant, or trio of dangerous louts, or at least no-one admitted to it.

"Who's the bailiff here?" Tuck asked as it neared midday and the pair were losing hope, despite furnishing themselves with warm savouries from a vendor. Tasty enough, even if they did find the claims of the filling being 'prime pork' to be rather dubious.

"Can't remember the fellow's name," John admitted. "But I've met him a couple of times over the years. He's alright."

"We should speak with him. If anyone will know about a giant who causes trouble, it'll be the local bailiff."

Edmund Vessey was the bailiff in Leeds, and he was a man of average appearance, his voice similarly bland. John had wondered in the past how such a man had risen to a position of authority, but Vessey was at least friendly towards the newcomers and seemed happy to help them. When the situation was explained to him and his outrage had been loudly voiced, John asked about the giant.

"A man like that would be well known," Vessey replied, shaking his head. "I mean, there's not many as big as you, John. That's why you get all the good bailiff jobs, while I deal with petty fines, and neighbours' arguing over a piece of land that the other's dog shit in!" He chuckled and the two companions dutifully joined in.

"You don't know him then?" Tuck asked hopelessly. "Haven't seen him here recently?"

John's heart sank at Vessey's words. If the fugitives hadn't come to Leeds, where the hell had they gone? They must be miles and miles away by now, far out of John and Tuck's reach. Little John might not have any claim on the stolen relic, or any great friendship with the assaulted priest in Pontefract, but the thought of such dangerous men roaming the streets did not sit well with him. He had hoped to bring them to justice and now it seemed those hopes had been utterly dashed.

"No, there's no one as tall as you living in Leeds," Edmund Vessey reiterated. "Unless they live like a hermit and never visit town. Which seems unlikely, considering what you say this fellow has got himself into, and how easily he deals out violence. A man like that doesn't go unnoticed for long."

"True," Tuck agreed. "So how is it we can't bloody find this man who should be well known to everyone for miles around?"

"Well, I said he doesn't live in Leeds," Vessey said, eyebrows raised and leaning into the friar as though he had a secret to share. "But there *is* such a man that's been living in York recently."

John and Tuck both straightened at that and, had they been dogs, their ears would have pricked up.

"York?"

"Aye, John, York. I've never seen him there myself – I don't travel much outside my own lands, you know. But I've heard rumours of a gang leader in York who's growing bolder with every day. He's been hiring all sorts of unsavoury types – veterans from the wars who're not afraid to rough people up to get their way."

"Those types have always thrived in the bigger towns and cities," Tuck noted sourly.

"Indeed," Vessey nodded. "But this fellow's been trying to control more and more of York's criminal underbelly – protection, prostitutes, kidnapping, extortion, gambling, that sort of thing."

"Stealing holy relics to sell to private collectors?" Tuck asked.

"That seems like exactly the kind of thing they'd do."

"Well, who is this gang leader?" John demanded. "Do you know his name? Where we can find him?"

Vessey held out his hands and smiled. "I told you, I don't travel much so I don't know York well. I've no idea where you can find the man, but I can tell you his name is William Wake, and he's hired the giant you asked about."

John took this in, sharing a pleased glance with Tuck. At last they had something else to go on, a new lead, and a good one at that, God willing.

"As I say, Wake has been more open recently. I've been told so by other bailiffs, and the headman in Tadcastre had some real trouble with him. Wake threatened to destroy the bridge over the River Wharfe if the villagers didn't pay him."

"What?" Tuck demanded. "That's outrageous!"

"I know!" Vessey cried. "That bridge is vital for trade – Tadcastre would be lost without it. But Wake must have some powerful people bribed, for no one stepped in to help the villagers and they were forced to pay Wake off."

John frowned, realising that perhaps this mission would not be as straightforward as he'd originally hoped. "If this Wake fellow is untouchable, how are we supposed to deal with him? There's only two of us and you're saying he's recruited what? An army of veteran soldiers?"

Vessey shrugged. "Maybe not quite an army, but aye, he has a few hard men working for him. That giant for one." He stood up and walked to the door of his house, peering out into the street as two children ran past playing some game, and a waggon rumbled by carrying barrels around to the rear of the manor house. "My advice to you two would be to head back to Pontefract and tell the bishop you lost the trail of these thieves. I know you're both used to dealing with violent men, and you're more than capable of dealing it out yourselves, but this can't end well for you, lads."

"That's not happening," John returned firmly. "There's a dying child who needs the healing power of that relic they stole. We're not turning back just because some criminal whoreson thinks he can act like a lord. Besides, anyone who can treat a priest like that needs stopped before they do worse."

Vessey raised an eyebrow and smiled warily. "Er, there's plenty of tales told about you boys where you did much worse than just kick priests in the face. I mean, didn't you punch a bishop, Tuck? And your old leader, Robin Hood, did the same."

"Aye, we did those things and more," Tuck agreed baldly. "But those clergymen were corrupt."

"They deserved it," John added. "We might have been outlaws, but we tried to do what was right. Besides, the men we're hunting murdered four innocent members of Pontefract's militia!"

Vessey nodded sheepishly, and it looked to John as though he was happy not to be punched himself for calling them out.

"Any other words of advice for dealing with this Wake and his lackeys before we head to York?" John asked him.

"I don't think anything I say would sway you one way or the other," Vessey smiled. "You know what you're about – who am I to advise you? But Leeds is quiet just now so, if you wish, I can let you take some of our town guards with you to try and retrieve that relic."

John broke into a wide grin and even let out a little cry of pleasure.

"That's very good of you," the friar said. "I'm sure Bishop Wulstan will be happy to hear about your helping us."

"Happy enough to pay my men's wages while they're with you?"

Tuck nodded, chuckling. "I'd say so."

John stretched out a huge hand and grasped Vessey's. "Thanks for this, Edmund," he said. "We won't forget it."

"Think nothing of it," the Bailiff of Leeds said airily. "If you can put William Wake and his lackeys in their place all England will be in your debt!"

CHAPTER EIGHT

Leeds was not beset by enemies, or even criminal gangs, but, even so, it was not a particularly large town, or very populous, and the bailiff did not have too many men to spare for John and Tuck's mission.

"There might only be four of us," the leader of these men said self-consciously to the famous former outlaws as they rode out of Leeds along the northeastern road to York. "But we know our business, you can count on that."

Tuck beamed at the four horsemen encouragingly. "We're happy to have you along, lads. You'll do for us, I'm sure of that."

John did his best to match the friar's enthusiasm but, in truth, Vessey's men were town guards, not proper soldiers. Maybe one or two of them had fought against the Scots, or in some other battles, but they'd let themselves grow fat around the middle and did not look like they'd fare well against the hardened, violent criminals they were hunting. Still, it was better than nothing and John mustered a smile for them before turning his attention back to the road.

The weather had grown even colder, and the bailiff took his hood from his pack and pulled it over his head, feeling relief almost immediately as his neck and face began to warm up. It was not windy, thank Christ, just bitterly cold and, as they rode, snow began to fall in thick, fat flakes.

"How far is it to York?" Tuck asked, also dragging his hood over his tonsured head and shivering as he squinted into the snow.

"About thirty miles as the crow flies," one of the guards told him. "The roads are well maintained so, normally, we'd make it there in good time. With this weather, though…" He trailed off and glanced irritably at the sky.

"You have tents?" John asked them. "In case we're forced to camp before we reach the city, or another village?"

"Aye, bailiff," their leader said, looking at his three companions almost like a proud parent. "We're well prepared for this, fear not. Tents, food, water, and weapons." He patted the sword that was hung on a baldric at his waist. "Hopefully the snow will let up though, eh?"

"I'll pray for it," Tuck said, clasping his hands around his mount's reins and bowing his head.

All external sounds seemed to fade as they travelled, the snow forming a cocoon around them so it was as if they rode through the countryside in a little world of their own. Jingling harness, snorting, trotting horses, and sniffling riders were the only things John could hear, and visibility was not much better.

"It's almost Christmastime," one of the guards observed, and John jerked upright, amazed to find he'd almost fallen asleep.

He sat straighter in the saddle and thought of his wife, Amber, back home in Wakefield. She would be getting things prepared for the Yuletide celebrations, he knew. Garlands of holly and ivy would be hung up on the houses, rich green leaves and red berries standing out in stark contrast to the white of frost and snow that blanketed the lands and the buildings. The mouth-watering scents of baking would fill the streets as folk like Amber made pies and other savouries using preserved fruit and meat. In the village tavern the patrons would tell ghost stories to one another as the fire blazed merrily, the door shut tight against the December storms. Will Scaflock, best friend to John and Tuck, would be alternating between cracking jokes and threatening to kill people. The bailiff smiled, wishing they'd brought Will along – even a giant wouldn't worry Will, who was widely known as Scarlet thanks to his vicious temper. But Will was in Wakefield seeing to his farm. At least John and Tuck would have a good tale to tell him, and all the other villagers when they returned home, hopefully in time to celebrate Christmas Day.

"Wake up, John!"

Friar Tuck was riding right beside him, and he shook his head woozily, realising he'd drifted off again. "I am awake," he protested, pulling down his hood, the frigid, icy air bringing him fully alert again.

"Just resting your eyes, eh?" Tuck asked with a sardonic laugh. "Well, we've all decided we need to stop and set up a camp before the weather gets any worse. These boys say there's a village not too far ahead but there's nowhere we could sleep, the place is only small. So we should get our tents up now."

John felt a little put out to have been bypassed in the decision making, but then he remembered he'd been dozing and thoughts of enjoying a happy Christmas with Amber and his friends chased away his irritation. "Good idea," he said, pointing a frost-rimed arm. "There's a likely stand of trees. We'll pitch our tents there."

The guards from Leeds might not look like the toughest fighters ever but they certainly knew how to set up a camp. Two of them had once been foresters and they regaled the others with tales of their days chasing outlaws as the tents were pitched, the horses settled for the night, wood gathered for a fire which Tuck got going, and water was collected from a nearby beck. The snow had not let up though and, although the mood was light, the men eventually grew somewhat morose as darkness settled in and thoughts of sleeping on the rock-hard ground filled their minds.

"How far are we from York now?" Tuck asked, not even looking up at the others as he stared fixedly into the fire, as though willing its warmth to chase away the snow. Even the bowl of hot porridge which John had made up for the friar did little to brighten him.

"Not too far," said the guards' leader, a very thin man named Ivor. "Maybe another seven miles or so. As long as the roads don't get completely snowed under we'll be there early tomorrow morning."

"And you're all ready to face a giant who's well versed in kicking the shit out of people?" John asked them while spooning steaming porridge into his mouth.

"We're fighting you?" one of the guards asked in an attempt at humour that fell flat.

"We're ready," the leader said firmly. "I told you, we know our business. We've dealt with hard men before. Leeds might not be York, and we might not have faced the likes of Robin Hood's gang, but we know which end of a sword is the sharp end."

John nodded, pleased by the conviction he heard in the man's voice, and the faces lit by the fire's flickering orange glow. "Good," he said, smiling around at them and glad to be rewarded with similar looks in return. Only Tuck seemed fed up with the journey through Yorkshire's snowy, December countryside, but John knew one sure way to cheer the friar.

"Tuck, why don't you give us a song. We'll join in."

Tuck's hooded face was hidden by shadows and the darkness that had swept inexorably over their camp with the setting of the pale sun. His eyes flashed though, and he asked, almost suspiciously, "A song? What song?"

"Well, it is almost Christmas," the bailiff replied. "How about getting us in the spirit of the season with that song you wrote yourself. What's it called again?" He knew the name of the song very well, for Tuck reminded everyone he'd written it every December, repeatedly.

"Ah, 'A Child Is Boren Amonges Man'," he said, and his face came up, glowing from more than just the firelight. "Excellent idea, John. You men might know this too," he told the guards proudly. "If you do, feel free to join in."

Little John enjoyed some carols, they certainly got one in the Christmas mood, but, and he'd never told Tuck as much, he'd never thought much of this particular song. There in the darkness though, with the snow falling and the other men's smiling faces, the bailiff felt a true sense of kinship and camaraderie. He joined in with Tuck, their voices combining in a rich, satisfying way that rolled out across the white-blanketed land.

Grinning, John helped the leader of the guards to refill his cup from a skin of ale that had been brought from Leeds, and, when Tuck's carol ended, the friar took up another that all were familiar with.

It was a surprisingly pleasant way to spend a December night outdoors, and John hoped his companions made the most of it, for there was a good chance they were all going to die when they rode into York the next day.

CHAPTER NINE

Hal winced as Grimbald punched the man again. Tanner wasn't really concerned about the violence, and the truth was the recipient of the blows had only himself to blame. And yet, there was a gleefulness to Grimbald's actions, a pleasure in dealing pain, that sickened Tanner.

"He's no good to you dead," he said.

Wake stared at the shuddering figure in the centre of the shadowy room. The man's face was covered in blood, and blood had trickled down to soak his woollen tunic. He had begged for clemency for a while, but he looked broken now, his cries only muffled sobs.

"Laurence has been of no use to me for months," Wake said, walking close to the bleeding man, bending down so that he could see him clearly. Laurence was tied to the sturdy chair and when he saw William Wake's face inches from his own, he flinched, as if he expected to be struck again. Wake just sighed. "How long am I to ignore your debt?" he asked.

"I will pay you what I owe," Laurence said, his tone whimpering. "You have my word on it."

Wake stroked at his beard.

"Ah, but you gave me your word that you would pay me six months since and where is my money?"

"Please, Sir," pleaded Laurence. "Please." Blood spattered from his lips as he begged. Wake stepped back, wiping flecks of spittle and blood from his cheeks in disgust. "My wife has been sick,"

Laurence continued. "My son—" his voice broke, his words turning to sobs.

"Yes, yes," said Wake, turning to the small window that looked out over the yard, "your son died. We know that sorry tale. I am not a heartless man. I did not chase you for payment these last two months. I gave you more than enough time to grieve, I think you will agree. Do you imagine you are the only man to suffer loss?"

"No, but... I..." Laurence sputtered. Not for the first time, Tanner felt sorry for him.

Two nights had passed since Tanner had returned to York. He had meant to leave the day before, but the steadily falling snow had been enough to deter him. That morning he had risen late, determined to set out for Ravenser Odd, when Laurence, a draper, had been dragged into the tavern by Roger and Robert, two burly brothers in William Wake's employ. Swirls of snow followed them in from the yard, reminding Tanner of the frigid journey that awaited him.

At first, Laurence had appeared to believe he might yet salvage the situation. He had fallen to his knees and implored Wake in the most pitiful manner. His brother, he had said, a tailor from Barnsley, was going to bring him the money to repay his debts, if only Wake would wait until after Yule.

"Alas," Wake had said, "I am not King Winter or Sir Christemas. Your time has run out." He waved a hand to the men who had brought Laurence in. "Take him upstairs."

Laurence had screamed for help as the two burly men hauled him to his feet and dragged him up the narrow staircase.

"Good thing you haven't left yet," Wake had said to Tanner with a smirk. "You can help with this."

Tanner had cast a glance at Raynald. If he had expected any kind of sympathy from the taverner, he was disappointed. Raynald scratched at his balding head and focused his attention on the carrots and onions on the chopping board. The message was clear: he had seen nothing, and Tanner knew he would hear nothing either, no matter how loud the sounds from the room above. Raynald had been the keeper of The Black Swan for decades. He knew better than to be observant when it came to his master's actions.

After Robert and Roger had tied Laurence to the chair, the brothers, no strangers to this upstairs room, had gone about hitting the man. Soon though, Wake had waved them away, making way for Grimbald. Now, the two stood near Tanner, silent and brooding. Tanner liked the brothers well enough. They were straightforward, tough, loyal and dependable.

Tanner pushed himself away from the wall, stepping into the dimly lit room. Even though it was day, a couple of rushlights burnt on the table against the gloom. The snow was thick on the roofs he glimpsed through the small window. It was still falling hard, cloaking the world in white. It gave the impression of cleanliness, hiding the muck of the city.

"Can you at least pay some of what you owe now?" Tanner said.

Laurence craned his head in an attempt to look at the owner of this new voice, but from where he was tied he could not see Tanner. The draper nodded his head furiously.

"Yes, indeed, good sir," he said. "God bless you. Indeed that is what I was saying to those brothers when they came to speak with me. I can pay a fifth-part of my debt now. The rest will be paid in full after Twelfth Night, when my brother arrives."

Wake spun about, turning his back to the window. His face was wreathed in shadows, but Tanner saw his eyes flash with anger.

Tanner bit his lip. Why was he trying to help this man? Laurence was nothing to him. It was dangerous to cross Wake and such defiance would gain him nothing.

"A fifth, you say?" said Wake, his tone unusually soft.

"Yes. At least a fifth." Laurence's tone grew expectant. "By God, my wife told me I was a fool to have borrowed from you. But I could see no other way."

Wake chuckled.

"Your good wife sounds like a clever woman. How long have you been bound in wedlock?"

"She is a good woman, my Helena," said Laurence, allowing a small smile. "Truly, I am blessed. We were wed sixteen years ago, on Saint Matthew's eve."

"Well," said Wake, "Helena was right to warn you not to borrow from me. After so long, she knows you well."

"Yes, but she does not know you, Sir," replied Laurence. Blood trickled from his nose and he sniffed. "That is to say, apart from your reputation."

"I am not sure what reputation that would be," said Wake. "Am I reputed to be a fair man?"

Laurence looked shocked. "Why, yes, of course."

"A man not to be trifled with?"

"Everyone knows not to cross you."

Wake's eyes narrowed. "So, I am feared?"

Laurence swallowed.

"Respected," he said, licking blood from his lips.

"Respected," replied Wake. "That is good. But respect comes from a certain amount of fear, wouldn't you agree?"

Laurence shrugged nervously. "Perhaps."

"Your Helena fears me," Wake said. "And she knows you well. That is why she warned you against borrowing what you could not repay."

"I can pay you a fifth now," Laurence said, his voice small, as if he sensed the conversation had moved on, leaving him stranded and lost. "Perhaps even a quarter."

"I don't dislike you, you know?" Wake said. "In fact, I rather like you. You have an easy way about you, Laurence, even now, tied to a chair and bleeding, you speak well, making sound offers."

Despite his precarious situation, Laurence smiled.

"Thank you, Master Wake," he said. "I try to be genial in all my dealings. I am sorry there has been this unpleasantness between us. I know I brought it on myself."

"I am sorry too," said Wake. "I don't really care about the money you owe. It is a pittance." He waved a hand airily. "A sum barely to be noticed."

On hearing these words, Laurence visibly relaxed.

"Oh, sir, I am so glad to hear you say such. I told Helena you would see reason."

William Wake scowled, as if confused.

"Oh, no," he said, shaking his head. "Wise Helena was right all along. It is not about the sum, you see. It is about respect."

"You have my full respect, sir."

"Fear too?" asked Wake. "Are you scared of me?"

Laurence squirmed uncomfortably. "Well, I would not wish to lie to you. Tied as I am to this chair and sorely beaten by your men, I must admit I was frightened. For a time."

"For a time," Wake echoed. He looked up at the darkened rafters for a moment. "Alas, however much I like you, Laurence, I cannot let you leave here, unless you have all that you owe me hidden in your braies."

Laurence gave a nervous laugh. Tanner's heart sank. He had sensed that, like a cat that has caught a vole by the river, Wake had only been playing with the poor man.

"Well," snapped Wake, all trace of humour gone, "do you?"

Laurence looked truly confused and pathetic. "Sir?"

"Do you have a few groats hidden up your arse?"

Laurence swallowed. He tried to smile, but the expression refused to come and he looked pained instead.

"You know I do not have your money."

"So, it is as I thought and as good Helena feared. You cannot pay me, and if I am to retain the respect of those who do business with me, I must make of you a warning; a message to any who think I will allow them to welch on debts."

"You said you liked me..." Laurence's voice withered into silence as he sensed the end of his path arriving.

Wake pouted, as if sad.

"Oh, and I do. Which is why I do not wish to do the deed myself." Grimbald stepped forward, happy to whatever Wake commanded. Wake halted him with a raised hand and turned his cold gaze on Tanner. "No, Grim," he said. "You've had your fun. This job falls to my *partner*." He said the word with a sarcastic twist. Pulling a short-bladed knife from a sheath at his belt, he held it out to Tanner handle first. "Hal, cut this poor bastard's throat."

CHAPTER TEN

Tanner didn't move. Laurence let out a choked whimper. Hal didn't look at him. His eyes were locked on Wake and the blade in his hand. The metal of the knife glimmered in the glow of the rushlight flame. There was a wicked gleam in William Wake's eyes.

"Come on, Hal," he whispered, "you need to be on your way. Once you are done with Laurence, Rob and Rog can get rid of the body."

Laurence's whimpering turned to panting gasps. His words tumbled out in a panicked rush.

"I will pay you. I can send word to my brother and have him come right away."

The draper continued pleading, sobbing and moaning. Wake ignored him. To him, the man was already dead.

Tanner stared into Wake's soulless eyes. He wondered if his own eyes looked like that. Was he destined to become such a man? Was he already? How had it come to this? He had no qualms with killing men who opposed him, or meant him harm. On the road from Pontefract, the men from the hue-and-cry had taken up arms and ridden against him. They were enemy combatants. Johannes too had been warned. He was no innocent. He had made his own decisions, knowing the consequences. The weeping draper, thrashing against his bonds so frantically now that he risked toppling the chair, had made a foolish mistake. He had borrowed money from an unscrupulous man and now found himself unable to repay his debt.

Did he deserve to die for that? And after his son had been snatched from him.

Tanner scowled as the sudden stabbing memory of May's death hit him. He tried to keep those memories pushed far down where they seldom surfaced, but seeing the girl on the wagon at the city gate had stirred the murky depths of his mind. He recalled Katerina's anguish at their daughter's death even more acutely than his own despair. He had been powerless, unable to lessen her pain. It was his guilt that had driven the wedge between them.

"Take the knife, Hal," Wake said. A furrow had appeared between his eyes. He did not blink.

Tanner did not move.

"Surely there is a better way than this," he said. "They've just lost their son. Think of the man's poor wife."

"Yes," moaned Laurence. "Think of my wife."

Neither man looked in his direction. William Wake continued staring into Tanner's eyes. His gaze sharpened.

"Have you gone soft on me, Hal?" he said. "I never thought I'd see the day."

"I haven't gone soft," Tanner replied. "I just don't like killing needlessly. It's too messy."

"Don't you worry about the mess. Raynald will mop the floors."

"You know what I mean. This will bring too much attention on you. On us both."

"Nonsense. You heard what I said. This is about respect. Fear, and respect. Now," he shoved the knife towards Tanner, "take the damn knife and do what I have commanded of you. Or perhaps I should seek a new partner."

Behind Wake, Grimbald grinned, his teeth like yellowed tombstones in the tangle of his beard.

There was a smile on William Wake's face too, but his eyes showed his true mood. He was furious. Tanner understood the test he now faced. He was acutely aware of Robert and Roger standing behind him. Both of them were strong, able, and carried blades on their belts. Then there was Grimbald, who would be more than eager to kill Tanner if he was given the order. Tanner swallowed. If he failed this test, he would be dead in moments. Or worse, he would find himself tied to that same chair. In either case Laurence would still die, by his hand or another.

"You don't need a new partner," he said and reached out his hand for the knife.

Before he could take the blade, Laurence, who had fallen silent for a time, let out a scream of such volume that it startled all the other men in the small room.

"Help me!" he bellowed. "By the grace of God, help me! They mean to murder me!"

For an instant, nobody moved. Until that moment, Laurence had given no indication he could make such a noise. He had wept and whined, but nobody would have heard him beyond the walls of the tavern. Now, his voice was as loud as thunder, as piercing as a crowing cockerel.

The initial shock of his booming shouts evaporated quickly. Grimbald stepped forward, no doubt to deliver a blow to silence the man. But before he could punch Laurence, the draper's screaming halted abruptly. It was replaced by gurgling, wheezing, gasping cries. Blood fountained from the severed artery in his throat, spraying Grimbald in gore. The giant stopped in his tracks, as if he'd been slapped.

Tanner blinked. His hand was still outstretched, but he would not be needing the knife now. Wake had seen to that. He stepped back quickly from the dying man, avoiding the worst of the blood gushing from the deep gash he had drawn across the man's throat with the sharp blade.

"There," Wake said, looking down at Laurence, who grunted and mouthed in agonised horror. "If only you had not gone so soft, Hal, we could have avoided that." He massaged his temples with the fingers of his left hand. "I have a headache now."

Tanner glared at Wake, but kept silent. Grimbald wiped a meaty hand over his face, smearing blood into his beard. One of the brothers, Roger, Tanner thought, let out a snorting sound that might have been a laugh, or a sob.

"Perhaps we can get on with our day now," said Wake, wiping his knife's blade on the shoulder of Laurence's tunic. He was about to say more, but before he uttered another word, there came a commotion from the room below.

"In the name of the mayor, let us pass!" The voice was crisp and loud, with the ring of command.

Grimbald shot a look through the window to the yard.

"Half a dozen of the Watch," he said. "More inside already from the sound of it."

It was true, there was the sound of crashing from below as furniture was overturned. Men shouted. Raynald's rasping voice rose above the din.

"You have no right to barge in here."

"We have every right!" replied the first voice. "We are in pursuit of a thief. Now we hear screaming for help from the upper floor. Step aside!"

"I'm no thief," came a third voice. With a start, Tanner recognised it as belonging to Dick Blount. What in the name of all that is holy had that fool got himself in now?

The sounds from below grew louder, with other voices added to the tumult. Shouts and demands were met with further angry shouts and refusals.

Snapping out of the stillness that had momentarily gripped him, Tanner moved quickly to the stairs. No matter what he thought of Wake and what had transpired here, he had set his course with him and there was no time to contemplate or to plan next steps.

"Will," Tanner snapped, "we have prepared for this. Take Grim and get out of here. Rog and Rob, you stay with me. We'll hold them off as long as we can."

Grimbald was already moving to the rear of the room. Tanner was glad he did not argue. Whatever else, Grimbald was capable of following orders. Throwing open a chest, he pulled out a length of rope. Large knots dotted the rope at two-foot intervals. William Wake seemed to be rooted to the floor. Grimbald was looping the rope about a stout hook Tanner had had fitted into one of the building's beams. He had hoped never to have to use the rope or the hook, but he had made all the men within the inner circle of Wake's organisation train for just such an occasion.

"Will," he said, his voice as sharp as a sword thrust, "if you are caught here now," he flicked his glance at Laurence's blood-soaked corpse, "we'll all hang. We'll buy you time to get to the arranged place. If we are not there by nightfall, set off towards Ravenser Odd. If we are alive, we'll find you there."

Below, the shouting had changed into something else. Men still yelled and insulted each other, but now there was a more dangerous edge to those voices. Wake stared at him for a heartbeat. The unmistakable sound of blades clashing reached them.

"Go!" Tanner said.

Snatching up the saddlebags that as far as Tanner knew still held the relic, William Wake hurried to where Grimbald stood beside the window. This window looked down into a narrow alley and was usually left shuttered. Being so close to the building opposite, it was of scant use for letting in light. Wake had paid a carpenter to put it in at Tanner's insistence. He had complained of the expense then. He was not complaining now.

Grimbald had thrown open the shutters. Freezing wind blew in, shivering the flames on the rushlights. Grimbald flung the knotted rope out of the window and offered his hand to Wake to help him over the sill. The window was not large. Tanner knew it would be a tight squeeze for the brute, but they had made sure he could fit, not that Tanner cared if the brute should be caught here.

To the saddlebags, Wake had added a large sack, a scabbarded sword, and belt, and a cape and hat that he had grabbed from where they hung on the wall. All of these items he now tossed out the window.

"You should come with us now," Wake said, throwing a leg over the sill and grasping the rope. "You'll hang, if you stay."

The clash of weapons was loud from the door to the landing. A man cried out in pain. It sounded to Tanner as if Raynald and Dick were losing ground and the fighting had moved to the stairs themselves.

"I'll catch up with you," Tanner said. "Now flee."

Drawing his sword, he moved to the door. Robert and Roger waited expectantly, weapons already in their hands.

Wake began to lower himself down the rope, but hesitated just before his head dropped below the window ledge. The snow was falling so fast that flakes already dotted his hair and beard.

"Hal," he said.

Tanner's hand was on the door handle. He glanced back at Wake.

"You're right," Wake said. "You haven't gone soft, have you?"

Tanner didn't bother answering. Taking a breath, he nodded at the two brothers, pulled open the door and headed down the dark stairs.

CHAPTER ELEVEN

Descending the stairs, Tanner walked into chaos. As his eyes adjusted to the gloom, he took a moment to assess what was happening. The slim figure of Richard Blount was closest to him, in front of the boy stood the solid shape of Raynald. The taverner had positioned himself at the bottom of the stairs behind a makeshift barricade comprised of a bench, a stool, and an overturned table. Tanner took a step down and realised there was something else blocking the way to the stairs: the body of a man, sprawled over the bench. The man appeared to be dead. He was garbed in the blue livery of the City Watch. There was blood on the rush-strewn floor beneath him.

Blount turned at Tanner's approach. From the expression on the youth's face, he knew he was somehow responsible for all of this.

"What did you do?" Tanner hissed. But there was no time to talk. Before Blount could respond, Tanner shoved him aside. "We're with you, Ray."

Raynald grunted. In his hand he held a stout cudgel, the knobbly wood polished smooth. Tanner knew that Raynald had once fought with the old King Edward at Flanders. He had heard he was a skilled archer too, his broad back and shoulders testament to the countless hours with the longbow at the butts. But his days of soldiering were far in the past and Tanner had never seen him do more than call for help when patrons grew too rowdy. Tanner's appraisal of the man changed in an instant.

Enraged at the sight of their fallen comrade, the other guards, six in all, surged forward, urged on by their leader, a grey bearded man-at-arms. Raynald did not flinch as they advanced. They had clearly had time to coordinate their attack. Four of them swung their swords over the table and bench, while the other two set about dragging the barricade out of the way.

Any hope Tanner might have had of talking or bribing their way out of this fled. This had gone far beyond talk and neither he nor Wake had enough money to pay off the murder of a city guard. Tanner still had no idea what had sparked this sudden violence, or why the guards were there in the first place. He would think about that later. If he survived. Now, all he could do was fight and hope he could contain this mess.

Beside him, Raynald feinted away from a sword thrust, then brought his club down on the man's wrist. The guard shrieked, dropping his blade and falling away from the fight, toppling one of the other men at the same time. Tanner dodged a man's wild swing, swaying out of the blade's path, then pierced the guard's gambeson with the point of his sword. Tanner was not thinking now, he was fighting as he had trained to do since he was a boy. He had ever been deadly with a sword in his hand and now was no different. He twisted his blade, feeling his assailant's shiver through his sword's steel. It was a killing blow. Tanner knew that instinctively. Dragging his sword free, the guard collapsed.

The other men were hesitant now. They had hauled the table and bench out of their path, but three of their number had fallen and their blood was thick on the floor. The man-at-arms was bellowing at them, but some of these men had never tasted real combat before and they were wary.

Tanner glanced at Raynald. The man still held his cudgel aloft, standing defiant at the bottom of the stairs. But as he looked, Tanner's heart sank. Four against the two of them had proven too much. Blood bloomed on the taverner's tunic. Looking down, Raynald saw it too.

"Bastards," he spat.

"Can you yet fight?" Tanner asked.

"It will take more than these whelps to stop me," growled the old man.

The man-at-arm's shouts had finally cut through his men's fear and they regrouped. If the watchmen rushed them now, they had a good chance of prevailing against the two defenders. With the barricade in place, only Raynald and Tanner had been able to fight, now Tanner saw a chance to even the odds.

Behind the guardsmen, the door stood open. The light from the yard was bluish and as cold as the snow that fell in fluttering silence. Adam was there, peering into the tavern. His bruised face was a mask of terror and shock at what he was witnessing. Tanner could barely believe the boy had not already fled. He was a brave one, for sure. Perhaps brave enough to do one last thing before he ran away and saved himself from the repercussions of what was happening here.

"Adam!" Tanner shouted, his voice cutting through the noise in the room, as the guards readied themselves to charge. "Shut the door and block it. Then run!"

For the briefest of moments Adam stared at him in disbelief. The man-at-arms too, gaped in grim horror as he understood the implication of Tanner's order. He turned to prevent the stablehand from carrying out the command, but he was too late. Adam slammed the door and the grey-bearded warrior's fist pummelled the wood futilely. He roared at the boy to open up.

The door did not budge. Tanner let out a breath. The boy was as resourceful as he was brave it seemed. Tanner did not know what Adam had used to block the door, but whatever it was, it was enough to make the man-at-arms give up his attempt at opening it and turn back to the room. With the door shutting out the cool light, the tavern was now even gloomier than before. The guards eyed the men on the stairs with a mixture of hatred and fear. The man-at-arms stepped forward to join his men, reluctantly dragging his own sword from its scabbard. Tanner could see the grim determination in that grey-whiskered face. He knew as well as Tanner that this would end now, one way or another.

Raynald understood it too. He stepped away from the stairs, making room for the others. Tanner moved with him, never taking his eyes off the guards.

"Rog, Rob, Dick," he said. "Now's the time to earn your keep."

The two brothers came down the stairs quickly and joined Raynald and Tanner. Dick faltered.

"What are we going to do?" he asked.

"If any of them leave here, we all hang," Tanner said. "You wanted to fight, now draw your sword and get down here!"

Still, Dick did not move.

The man-at-arms, seeing the momentary indecision in the defenders, barked an order at his men. They rushed forward, clearly determined to overrun them. Tanner cursed.

Dismissing Richard Blount from his mind, Tanner roared his own command, springing forward to meet the charging guardsmen. He was pleased to see that Raynald, Roger and Robert came with him. Then the room was once again filled with the clashing of steel and the shouts to fighting men, and Tanner gave himself up to the terrible joy of battle.

CHAPTER TWELVE

"Stop your whimpering," snapped Tanner. "You'll live." He didn't say anything else, instead leaving his words hanging in the air like a smell to add to that of smoke from the hearth and the sour stink of blood and shit.

Dick sat on the steps, his pallid face streaked with tears. He cuffed at his cheeks, looking about at the devastation in the tavern. It was quiet now, the sudden hush seeming to echo in their ears after the tumult of the fight.

Tanner knelt beside Raynald. The old man grimaced in pain. His eyes shone. He drew in shallow breaths.

"Told you those boys couldn't stand against the likes of me," he said, grunting as a wave of pain gripped him.

"You did well," Tanner said, looking at the corpses in the room. Raynald had killed one of them before the man-at-arms had stabbed his sword under the taverner's guard. Tanner had seen the warrior's sword plunge into the old man's guts. With a cry, he had fought his way to Raynald's side, punching another man out of his way.

"Well?" Raynald said, coughing up a spume of blood. "Well? I held on to that bastard's sword long enough to allow you to finish him." He grinned at the memory, his teeth red with blood.

"You're a tough one," said Tanner. "No man could deny that."

Raynald had seen Tanner coming to his aid and had twisted his body to the side, making it awkward for the man-at-arms to free his sword from his flesh. Tanner had reached them a moment later, hacking his sword into the man-at-arms' exposed head, killing him instantly. But not before the man-at-arms had in turn killed Raynald. The taverner was as dead as the commander of the guards, the wound was merely taking longer to claim him.

"Don't be so hard on the boy," Raynald said, leaning back and closing his eyes. His tunic was drenched in blood and his skin was sallow. "He is brave," he whispered.

"Brave?" hissed Tanner. "If he had come when I'd called, you might live."

Dick had hesitated at the top of the stairs as the battle raged. His wide eyes had told the tale of his fear, but when Raynald had fallen, the young man had thrown himself at the guards with a shriek of horrified fury, slicing and hewing at them. His savage attack, coupled with the death of their leader saw the watchmen's morale shatter. The fight was over soon after. The last two guards threw down their weapons, crying out for clemency.

They received none. In a welter of blood, Roger and Dick cut them down. A further two guards had been badly wounded. They moaned and shouted out for aid. Roger killed them with quick cuts of his sword.

"It is brave to fight when you are terrified," said Raynald. His voice was no more than a whisper now. "The boy did well." He fell silent and Tanner thought he had gone. Above Dick's sniffling weeping came the sound of Roger's voice, trembling anguish softening his usually gruff tone.

"Don't leave me," he said, shaking Robert's shoulder. "Don't you dare." He had thrown aside his sword and sat beside his brother. Robert's head lolled, his mouth open, eyes staring.

"How does Rob fare?" Raynald's voice startled Tanner. The taverner's eyes fluttered open. His chest barely rose and fell now. Tanner shook his head. As if Roger had been watching him, he let out a strangled wail of grief.

"No use sitting by my side," Raynald said. "We both know I'll be joining Rob soon enough." Tanner wanted to say something comforting, but looking down at the blood-drenched tunic, he knew Raynald was right. "Go now," Raynald went on. "Or I'll have died for naught. If you stay here, you will have your necks stretched within the week."

Tanner bit his lip. He didn't want to leave Raynald on his own. It wasn't right. He opened his mouth to say as much, that he would sit with the old man for a time and then leave, when he saw the decision had been taken from him. Raynald's eyes were open still, but the light of life had faded from them. A rattling sigh escaped his lips as his mouth fell slack. Tanner pushed Raynald's eyelids closed.

"Raynald was right," he said, sweeping his gaze about the room. His eyes lingered on the crying youth on the stairs. "About all of it." For the first time he noticed the blood on Dick's sleeve. "How bad is it?" he asked.

Dick pulled up his sleeve and appeared shocked when he saw the long cut on his left arm. He gritted his teeth, the pain coming with the realisation he'd been injured. From where Tanner stood, it didn't look that bad. Painful yes, but not dangerous.

"Roger," Tanner said, "bind Dick's arm. Both of you, be ready to leave as soon as you are done with that wound. Take the warmest clothes you can find, and anything of value you can carry. And get some provender from the larder. There's no telling when we will be able to stop for food."

Shaking his head like a dog stepping from a stream, Roger pushed himself to his feet.

"Where are we going?" he asked.

"There's no time for questions now," replied Tanner. "Do as I say and be ready to leave."

He didn't wait to see if Roger had obeyed him. If Rog and Dick chose to oppose him, they could go to hell. He would be out of the city and ahead of the news of the death of the guardsmen, no matter what these two fools did.

Hurrying over to the fireplace, he reached a hand inside the chimney. The stone was hot to the touch, but not unbearable. He had never once opened this secret hiding place when anyone else could see him and he was acutely aware that Roger and Dick were both watching him intently. They could both be damned. It mattered nothing to him now that they should see his hiding place. He would never be coming back to The Black Swan.

Sliding out the loose brick, he let it tumble into the smouldering coals, sending up a cloud of ash and a spray of sparks. He would usually have been careful not to make a noise, but there was no need for stealth now.

He reached tentatively into the gap where the brick had been. The metal inside was not hot.

There was scant space within the hole for his hand, and he awkwardly prised out the object within, careful not to drop it and spill its contents. He drew out into the dim light a plain iron box. It was solidly made, but simple. A smith from Pocklington had made it for him to his exact specifications. Tanner had not dared have any of the craftsmen of York fashion the box for him, for fear that Wake would learn of its existence and question him about it. This had been his secret since beginning to work with William Wake. Every few weeks when The Black Swan was quiet, in the dead of night, he had carefully hidden away some of his coins within the box. There was by no means a fortune within, but it would be enough for him to start fresh somewhere far from here. He would take Roger and Dick with him if they wanted to come. There was safety in numbers on the roads. If they wanted to part ways when they reached London or Bristol, or wherever he decided to settle, he cared not a whit.

He lowered the box to the flagstones beside the hearth. Even before he opened it, he knew something was wrong. It was too light by far. Holding his breath, he removed the lid and saw what he had feared. It was empty.

A sudden rush of fury gripped him. He threw the lid into the fire with a clatter. Who had known the box was there? He could almost hear Katerina's snide voice whispering "They that sleep with dogs, shall rise with fleas." Perhaps he did deserve all the misery that had befallen him, but to think he had risked everything for William Wake, helped him escape and in doing so had murdered guards of the City Watch, filled him with a searing rage.

A sudden thought came to him and he looked over at the men on the stairs. Roger was bandaging Dick's arm with a strip of linen he had found somewhere. Dick was sitting rigidly, holding his arm out for Roger and purposefully looking away from his injury. The youth was watching Tanner with open curiosity. Roger was concentrating on his task of binding the boy's cut, but on hearing the clangour of the iron lid, he had looked up. Tanner returned their gaze for a moment, searching for signs of duplicity. He saw none. Neither showed any sign of fear of him. They both knew what had happened to Johannes. They would not steal from him and expect there to be no reprisals. Pushing himself up with a grunt, Tanner stalked into the small storeroom where Raynald kept the food he served.

He began rummaging through the items on the shelves, in chests and hanging from the soot-dark beams. He half-hoped he would find his money hidden behind the ingredients in the storeroom, but dismissed the idea immediately. Raynald was many things, but Tanner did not believe he was a thief, at least not from a friend. He didn't know how Wake had found out about his secret stash of coins, but it seemed clear to him now that William was the most likely candidate to have stolen from him. The man would happily skin his own mother to make a few shillings.

In the storeroom, he found half a ham, some bread, a large slab of hard cheese, and a few onions and leeks. He had also found a skin and filled it with Wake's favourite Rhenish wine. All of these he tossed into a sack he had retrieved from a hook on the wall, then returned to the main room of the tavern.

"Trouble?" asked Roger.

"No more than we were already in." Tanner chose not to elaborate on the empty box and his flash of anger. Roger and Dick might not be the cleverest of men, but even they could read the meaning behind what they had witnessed. "Are you ready?"

Both Roger and Dick had donned thick hooded cloaks. Roger was going around the room, cutting the purses from all of the guardsmen. He poured the coins into the largest of the pouches that had been worn by the man-at-arms. He handed it to Tanner.

"Should pay our way for a few days at least," Rog said. His eyes were red and he had a haunted look about him, but he was a steady one. Tanner clapped him on the shoulder.

The pouch was quite heavy. Mainly pennies and farthings, Tanner was sure, but better than nothing. He added the pouch to the sack and handed the bag to Roger, who was taller and broader than him.

"Thanks for that," he said. "Sorry about Robert."

Roger nodded grimly, taking the sack without comment and slinging it over his shoulder.

"Where are we headed?" he asked.

Hal's momentary plans of travelling far away to start afresh in another city had been sundered with the discovery of the empty box. Now there was only one course of action that made sense, a path that could, with luck, see him profit from the risks and sacrifices he had made these last few days. He might even get back the money that had been stolen from him.

"We'll head out of the city as fast as we can. Then we'll make our way to a place Will and I arranged a long while ago."

"And then?"

"We shall see, but Will still has what we took from the church in Pontefract. Our best chance is to sell it as planned."

The money they were expecting from the sale of the relic would be enough for him to finally set up a new life for himself far from York. He could be done with William Wake once and for all.

He did not mention the nagging fear that Wake might not have waited for them as arranged and that the coins from his hidden box might not be the only things Wake had stolen from him.

CHAPTER THIRTEEN

The rest of the journey to York proved fairly uneventful. The snow continued to fall but intermittently, so it was not too deep for the horses to trot freely. There were patches of ice though, and that slowed the riders, for they feared their mounts slipping and possibly breaking a leg. Still, even with the harsh conditions, they arrived in York by mid-morning and John, Tuck, and the four guards from Leeds began the search for their quarry.

Asking at the city gates did not provide much useful information, as the guards denied any knowledge of the three fugitives. Even when John described the giant, demanding to know if the guards had seen a man of that size, they professed ignorance.

"Those bastards were lying," the bailiff growled as they stood with their horses, wondering where to start. "They knew exactly who we were looking for."

"Aye, you could see it in their faces," Tuck agreed. "You think they'll warn Wake that we're looking for him?"

"Possibly. It will depend on how much he's been paying them. Or perhaps how much they fear him. If they're genuinely worried that he might harm them if they don't do his bidding, maybe they'll be glad we're here to deal with him."

"You!" Ivor, leader of the men from Leeds, jerked his head towards a middle-aged, grimy looking fellow, gesturing him to come over. The street was quite busy and the man eyed them with great suspicion before silver coins glinted in Tuck's hand and then he came quickly, shoving his way through the other pedestrians and almost being run over by a peddler's waggon.

"Have you heard of William Wake?" Tuck asked, showing the shillings more plainly to the man, whose eyes grew wide before he regained control and made his expression blank.

"No, don't think so," the fellow said, obviously afraid to tell them what he knew, but too tempted by the friar's money to simply walk away.

"Are you sure?" John demanded. "What about a giant warrior, as big as me?"

"A lad like that would be hard to miss," said the man, rubbing a hand across his greasy chin.

"He would. So have you seen him? Or do you know where we might find him?"

The fellow's mouth opened and he licked his lips, eyes fixed on the coins that could be his if only he offered some useful information. He turned and looked about at the people bustling past them, still licking his lower lip, then stared at the four shillings once more and nodded.

"I think there's a big lad like that living on the other side of the river," he murmured, tilting his head so he could look around, still wary of being overheard. "Cross over the bridge and ask someone there. Like I say, such a big lad is hard to miss. You'll find someone over the bridge that knows where you can find him."

Tuck gazed at him for a moment, as though weighing up if his tip was worth the money, but, at last, he slipped it into the man's hand and it disappeared, as did their informant, who hurried away, quickly fading from sight amongst the other pedestrians, no doubt to spend his new wealth on a gallon or two of ale.

"If he told us the truth, our hunt is almost at an end," said John, eyes scanning the people of York who flowed past them, barely even registering the hard men in their midst.

"Over the bridge," Tuck nodded, gripping his quarterstaff and looking at the guards they'd brought from Leeds. "Are you boys ready? This could get very dangerous, very quickly. Wake may have a lot of support over the river."

The guards appeared nervous but each of them stood tall and nodded. They were armed, and they were ready. John examined each of them in turn and felt reassured – they'd not come to York for the scenery – the money they'd be paid for their service would be more than a year's wages and they were plainly determined to earn it.

"All right," the bailiff rumbled, mounting his horse again. Riding was discouraged in towns and cities, but few people would challenge six armed men, and John was in a hurry. "Let's go," he said. "Keep your hands close to your weapons, and be ready for anything. This isn't Leeds we're in now, it's a city, with dark alleys and dangerous cutthroats lurking in every shadow. And watch where your horse is stepping, the place will be filthy."

"Lead the way," Ivor growled, jaw set firmly and apparently doing his best to look as menacing as John.

There was no need for the bailiff to remind them all that York was a bustling, thriving city. The fact could not be ignored, for their senses were assailed at every step. Noise was everywhere, as animals were butchered in the streets, stonemasons hammered and thumped while building some new structure, and geese tied to vendors' stalls honked in alarm, trying desperately to break free. On top of all that, the smells of animal dung, sewage, offal, and fish merchants' wares assaulted the visitors' nostrils at every turn.

"Last night in the open, frosty air seems a thousand miles away from this," John noted, squinting in disgust as they passed a house with a pile of rotting garbage outside.

"Aye, cities are shit-holes," Tuck agreed. "I'll be glad when this is all over, and we can head home."

They reached the bridge over the Ouse soon enough and, as Tuck paid the toll with more coins from his purse, John asked the collectors about William Wake and the giant.

"The giant's name is Grim," one of the toll collectors told them openly enough, suggesting the name was common knowledge in that district.

"Grim?" John asked, not sure if he heard the man right.

"Aye, Grim, short for Grimbald de Pendok. Grim fits him perfectly!"

"Any idea where we might find them?" the bailiff asked.

That information was a step too far, and the toll collectors' shared that familiar, nervous look John had seen so often when hunting dangerous fugitives.

Another few shillings appeared from Tuck's purse and found its way into the collector's hand.

"You could try the Black Swan," the man said, and quietly gave them directions to the tavern, adding superfluously, "but I didn't tell you that."

"Thanks, friend." John nodded, and led the way across the river, staff held ready for whatever they might find there in William Wake's own area of the city.

This section of York did not stink as much as the one they'd just travelled through. There were less butchers and street vendors loudly hawking wares, but more taverns, and more unsavoury-looking characters hugging the shadowy walls of buildings, seemingly without purpose.

"Keep a hand on your coin purse," John advised his men, glaring at one of the loungers until the shifty fellow turned away.

"Down here, is it?" Tuck asked, pointing to an alleyway on the right. "I think that's what the toll collector said."

"Aye," John agreed. "We're nearly there. Remember, we're not here to start a fight, but if this Wake arsehole won't give up the relic, well, skulls might need cracked. Be careful though, lads. Don't forget these bastards have already killed four men who tried to bring them to justice."

"Who's taking the giant?" Tuck asked innocently.

"Him!" All four of the guards replied at once, nodding towards John who gave a sardonic laugh in response.

They fell silent as their mounts carried them further along the alley. The buildings rose up on both sides, making John feel claustrophobic. Although it was only around midday it had been gloomy even before they came into the oppressively compact alleyway and the six men scanned the shuttered windows and doorways for signs of danger.

"Think that's the place?" Ivor asked as they neared the midway point of the thoroughfare.

"I think there's a good chance of it, considering we're looking for a tavern called The Black Swan, and there's a great bloody sign hanging outside that tavern in the shape of a black swan."

Ivor laughed along with his men, and surreptitiously made an obscene gesture at Little John as they warily moved onwards, hands grasping staffs or loosening swords in scabbards, ready to be drawn in an instant.

The alley opened up into a courtyard and the gates were wide open, so the group rode inside. There were stables on the left but they were empty, and no one was around. Highly unusual, especially for that time of day.

Clearly, something was amiss.

The bailiff dismounted and the others did the same, quickly tethering the horses to the stables and taking their weapons.

They waited at the doors, listening but hearing nothing.

"It's as if the place is deserted," Tuck murmured, frowning as his eyes scanned the building. "Wait, look at this!" He went to the door and gestured at the handle. A thick-shafted broom had been forced through it, effectively locking the door, and trapping everyone inside.

"Not good," John said, leaning forward and pressing his ear against the door. "It's as silent as the grave in there. What the hell is going on?"

"Well, we're here now." Tuck grasped the broom and pulled, the wooden shaft scraping noisily against the door frame as it was drawn clear. "Ready, lads?" He peered up at the lowering sky, mouthed a quick prayer, and then he kicked open the door and threw himself inside.

"Good God!" Ivor was right behind the friar and he paused in shock to gape at the scene of carnage within the Black Swan. "This is insane! I've never seen anything like it!"

John followed him, taking in the sight that had turned Ivor's face as pale as the snow in the courtyard. Bodies lay strewn about the common room and, from the dark blue surcoats some of the corpses wore, it was clear they were city guards.

"Search the place," the bailiff commanded. "You two, take that side, Ivor, go through the back with him, Tuck, with me."

The men did not argue, following his orders immediately, glad to have something to do, and someone to take charge. Tuck was, of course, used to following John's lead for the massive bailiff had been Robin Hood's second-in-command when they were outlaws. The friar went up the stairs with John to the first floor, ready for anything.

"Poor bastard," the bailiff grunted as they came across the body of a man who'd been strapped to a chair and beaten black and blue before his throat had been carved open. "Not a nice way to go."

Tuck nodded and murmured a prayer commending the dead man's soul to God. "What do you think happened here?" he asked at last.

John shook his head and ran a hand across his face. "I think Wake and his lackeys were torturing this fellow for some reason, and his screams of pain brought the guards. Wake's men took on the lawmen, and then they all escaped through that window there before working their way back around to the stables and riding off." He pointed. "See how big it is? Even I could squeeze through there. It's been recently fitted too." John had been a blacksmith in his early life, and worked closely with carpenters, but he had never seen such a window. It had clearly been installed as an escape route for the gang members should the law, or rival criminals, ever come looking for them.

"Damn it!" Tuck cursed, dropping onto a stool and staring dully at the corpse in the chair opposite him. "What do we do now? Wake and the relic could be anywhere!"

John did not answer. He had no answer to give, for the friar was right. They'd done well to follow the thieves all the way to the Black Swan from Pontefract, but without any more leads to follow, it seemed the chase was over.

"Hal? Hal, sir?"

John and Tuck turned to one another in surprise as the high, reedy voice of a young boy filtered up to them from the front door.

"Hal, are you there?"

John bounded down the stairs and ran to the door which opened just a crack, revealing the frightened, grimy face of a youth. Seeing the enormous bailiff charging towards him, the boy turned and disappeared from view.

"Stop, in the name of the sheriff!"

John's huge palm slammed into the door, throwing it open with such force that one of the hinges snapped as he ran into the courtyard. He'd forgotten how slippery the ground was, coated in sleet and slush as it was, but so had the boy who skidded and fell in his desperation to escape.

"Come here, you!" John reached down and grabbed the lad under the arm, hauling him to his feet.

"No! I'm sorry, Grim! I did as Hal told me to do!"

"I'm not Grim," John said in a calm voice, reading the situation and sorry to have frightened the child so badly. "Look at me. I'm not Grim. I'm John Little. A bailiff."

That revelation did not reassure the boy as John had hoped it would. "Look, come back to the tavern. You're not in any trouble, and we're not going to hurt you, alright? Are you the stablehand? Aye, well I just want information from you. You'll be paid well, and then we'll be on our way."

His gentle tone, and the fact that he was not, after all, Grimbald de Pendok, did calm the youth's nerves somewhat, and, when they went back into the Black Swan, the kindly, round face of Friar Tuck set him even further at ease.

Ivor brought the boy some small beer and they gave him time to simply sit and rest, eyes wide as he looked around at the wrecked building and the dead bodies that littered the place. John knew this inn was probably the boy's home, and it must have been a horrible shock to see it in its present state.

Still, the relic and its thieves were getting further away by the heartbeat, and John had to find them.

"Who are you?" he asked the boy.

"Adam. I'm the stablehand."

"And who's Hal?"

"Hal?" the child's face became a blank mask.

"Don't play with me," John growled. "We heard you calling through the door for Hal."

"Hal is one of my master's...friends," came the reply.

"William Wake?"

"That's the master," the boy nodded.

"What happened here?" Tuck asked kindly.

The stablehand looked from friar to bailiff but the corpses of guards strewn about made it clear that this was far more trouble than even William Wake had been in before.

"You must tell us what you know," Tuck encouraged him with a sad smile. "Or the sheriff will think you had some part in it."

"Did you?" John asked. "Someone locked the door from outside."

The boy's face crumpled and he began to sob, eyes moving from one body to another before finally alighting on a man who did not wear a blue surcoat. "That's Raynald. Look what they did to him!"

"Adam, tell us why Raynald was killed, who Hal is, and where William Wake has gone," Tuck said, his voice becoming firm now, less friendly. "We have no time to waste, and if you help us, we will make sure the sheriff looks kindly on you."

Adam wiped the tears from his cheeks and sat up straight, rubbing his nose on a grubby sleeve. "Alright," he replied stoically. "I'll tell you. But Hal Tanner is a good man. He didn't cause all this...this killing. It's Wake and Grim that did it all." He trailed off, biting his lip, very clearly frightened, but he seemed to gather his courage and, after a long moment, went on again, telling them what he knew, and in what direction he'd seen the fugitives riding from his hiding place along the alley.

"Here," said Tuck, handing the boy some pennies. "Go and fetch the bailiff and the coroner and bring them here."

The child did not need to be told twice, and he snatched the coins before sprinting through the door, only slowing when he reached the snowy courtyard and remembered his earlier spill.

"Come on," John said, leading the men out to their horses. "We know which gate the bastards headed for, so let's get after them. Maybe we're not too late to catch up with them on the road."

"John?"

As they mounted their horses and made their way out of the courtyard, turning in the direction of Walmgate Barre, Ivor spoke up.

"Aye?" the bailiff said, glancing back at the man from Leeds.

"I know Hal Tanner. I served in the army with him."

John slowed his horse so he was riding beside Ivor.

"And? What's he like?"

Ivor shrugged. "I got on with him well enough. You could even say we were friends. I'm not really surprised he's got himself mixed up with the likes of William Wake though, he had a right nasty streak in him. He's dangerous, John, so we'll need to be careful. If it came to a fight, I think I'd rather face the giant than Hal Tanner."

"Well, make sure your sword is loose in its scabbard," the bailiff replied caustically, riding ahead to the front of the group again. "Because there's a good chance we're going to be fighting both of them soon enough, and Ivor?"

"Aye?"

"I don't care how dangerous these men are. If they stand in my way, they're going to regret it."

CHAPTER FOURTEEN

Tanner cursed under his breath. What a fool he'd been to imagine he would be able to rid himself of William Wake so easily. He wondered when Wake had found his stash of coins. Not that it mattered now. But the ramifications of the theft hung as heavily as the damp cloak about Tanner's shoulders. Wake must surely have decided Hal had outlived his use as his partner. Perhaps he would keep him alive until they reached their destination. There was safety in numbers on the road after all. But once they reached Ravenser Odd? What then? Tanner imagined Grimbald would accept the order to kill him with his usual glee at the prospect of inflicting suffering.

The snow had begun to fall more heavily now and Tanner kicked his horse into a trot. He thought it most likely that Wake wouldn't strike until Brough at the earliest, but of course, the easiest place to do away with your enemies without consequences was the road. A windswept road, crusted with ice and banked with snow along the hedgerows, provided the perfect opportunity for a quick murder. Tanner would have to watch himself. He looked back towards the walls of York. The city was grey and indistinct in the snow-swirled distance. Perhaps Wake did not even expect Tanner to escape the city. The truth was it had been a savage fight, and the three of them had been lucky to escape with their lives.

Tanner glanced at Roger, who rode with his head lowered, his hood hiding the anguished grief on his face. Beside him, shoulders hunched, and snow in the hair of his uncovered head, rode Dick. The young man's cheeks were red, his eyes shining. Tanner had already told him to pull his hood up or to wear a hat, but the boy had ignored him. Tanner wasn't about to tell him again. Dick was no child to be chided, and Tanner really did not care if the lad caught cold. But he vowed to himself that he would not slow his pace for the sake of the boy. Dick could take his own chances.

"Why'd you mention Brough?" Tanner snarled without warning, surprising himself with the vehemence in his words.

"I've said I'm sorry already," replied Blount, sounding more like a sulking child than ever. "It isn't as if those guards are going to come after us."

Tanner knew his anger was really aimed at himself for telling the others where they were going. He'd known it was a mistake as soon as he had spoken, but he had been shocked at how quickly Dick had let their destination slip. And to the city watchmen no less! It was true that Tanner had paid them a sizeable bribe to keep them quiet and, with the weather worsening, there was little chance anyone would be on their trail so soon, but it made their situation even more precarious. Tanner could feel the pressure of what they left behind them on the blood-soaked floor of The Black Swan and the looming presence of Wake and Grimbald ahead of them closing in on him.

"Are you such a fool, Dick?" Tanner spat the words. "Do you imagine the Watch will turn a blind eye to the death of their own? They *will* come after us. We can never return to York. We'll be lucky if we're not tracked down and swinging from a rope before Christmas Day."

Dick rubbed at his neck as if he could already feel the noose tightening. He glowered at Tanner, but was wise enough to remain silent now. They rode on into the falling snow, leaving the ice-draped walls of York behind.

The weather worsened, the sky darkening and thick curtains of billowing snow making visibility difficult. Roger said nothing, lost in his pain and perhaps reflecting on his own part in all this and what the future held in store for them. Even Dick tugged up his hood and pulled it tight about his ears against the cold. Tanner grimaced, but said nothing more. He scoured the horizon for any sign of a farmstead or a village. He wanted to put as far between them and York as possible and was even tempted to bypass Brough and make directly for Ravenser Odd, but they would have to pass the smaller settlement first and with the snow falling thick and fast and the chill wind shaking the branches of the trees in the fields, they could not hope to reach the Humber and Brough before they would need to seek shelter.

Tanner could no longer feel his fingers and he was beginning to lose hope of seeing anywhere suitable for them to rest when Dick let out a cry. The young man was pointing eagerly into the distance.

"What is it?" Tanner asked, seeing nothing at first save the grey, cloud-heavy sky and the waves of falling snow flakes.

"Smoke," Dick said. "There, in those trees."

Tanner peered, squinting against the chill wind. Dick was right. A dark smudge of smoke, no doubt from damp wood, rose up above a stand of spindly alders.

"Do you think it's them?" Dick asked.

"I don't know," said Tanner, unease making him shiver as much as the cold. "But I don't think we should just ride on up to a fire without checking what it is we're riding into. I've had enough fighting for one day."

"Come on, Hal," whined Blount. "Who else could it be out on a day like today. I'm freezing. Let's just see who it is."

"Shut up," snapped Tanner. "You will do as I say. If there is nothing to fear, I'll call for you in a moment. But if all is not well, better to be safe."

"I'm cold," Dick moaned.

Roger swung around to face the youth. He had not spoken since they had left The Black Swan. Now his eyes were red-rimmed, his lips pulled back from his teeth in rage.

"Do as you're told, boy," he growled. "You are alive still. The dead never get warm."

Dick had no answer to that. Nodding at Roger, Tanner dismounted.

"Don't wait on the road," he said, glancing back in the direction they had come. He saw nothing to indicate they were being followed, but the hairs on the back of his neck prickled. Something was not right. Danger was close. "Lead the horses over there." He pointed to a drystone wall and a shadowy shape of a holly tree. He could barely see them in the wintry gloom of the snowfall, but they would offer Dick and Roger some protection from the elements while they waited for him to return.

CHAPTER FIFTEEN

Tanner loosened his sword in its scabbard as he crept towards the trees. He clenched and unclenched his fists in an effort to return some feeling to his fingers. He wore gloves, but after riding through the snow, his hands were numb and he was worried that if it came to fight, he might drop his sword. The fresh snow crunched beneath his boots. The wind changed direction, shaking the bare branches of the alders so that they rattled like old bones.

A waft of woodsmoke blew in his direction, the scent conjuring images of warmth and welcome. Through the boles of the trees he could see that the fire was large, its flames leaping high and illuminating the trees. It was madness to have such a visible fire when on the run. Perhaps this conflagration did not belong to Wake after all. Still, whoever had lit the blaze, surely they would not begrudge sharing its warmth with other travellers on this dreary, freezing December day.

He was still some way off and he halted, scouring the stand of trees for signs of the fire's owner. An instant later, the unmistakable bulk of Grimbald came into view. He carried an armful of branches that he threw down near the fire. As Tanner watched, he took one of the largest of the boughs and tossed it onto the fire, causing the flames to jump in a spray of sparks.

Tanner drew in a deep breath. He was still unsure of the reception he would receive, but he was so cold he was almost beyond caring. The fire's warmth called to him. Wake was a tricky one, but had Tanner ever truly trusted him? He would keep his wits about him and, with luck, he would see a way to reach their destination with his life and, perhaps, even with the money that had been stolen from him. Wake was not the only one who could be cunning and ruthless.

Tanner was about to stand up and call for Dick and Roger to join him when a movement nearby caught his eye. He halted, peering into the gathering gloom and tried to make out what he had seen.

A dark shape was moving stealthily near the crumbling wall that ran down to the road. With a start, Tanner saw it was William Wake, wrapped in a dark cloak. Perhaps the man had stepped away from the fire to relieve himself, he thought. He had no desire to watch Wake squatting with his braes round his ankles, and was about to look away, but something in the man's stealthy movements tugged at his attention.

Unmoving, he watched as Wake picked his way along the wall until he found where snow had drifted against several fallen stones that had fallen from the top of the wall. Such damage to walls was common, and would be fixed by the local farmer when the weather improved. Wake crouched down beside the rocks, but rather than untie his hose, he looked furtively around, then began moving the stones aside.

Tanner hunkered down as low as he could, holding himself as still as if he had been made of ice. Wake gave no indication that he had seen him. With a final nervous glance all around, he pulled something from where it had rested over his shoulder. Even at this distance, Tanner recognised his own leather saddlebags. Wake deposited the bags into the hollow he had made, then quickly covered them with the stones and finally scooped snow back over the pile. With the snow falling so heavily, there would soon be no sign that the area had been disturbed.

No sooner had he hidden the saddlebags, than Wake rose and trudged quickly back through the snow towards the fire. Tanner heard his raised voice, followed by Grimbald's rumbled reply. Wake threw another piece of wood onto the fire and momentarily, both men were silhouetted against the flames. They were certainly making no attempt to hide their presence so close to the road.

Checking his sword again, Tanner waited a short while, then, when he began to shiver and the attraction of the fire grew too much to resist, he stood and strode towards the alders and the makeshift campsite.

"Hail the fire," he called out as he approached.

There was a moment's pause, then Wake's voice came through the gusts of wind and snow.

"Is that you, Hal?"

"Who else?" Tanner shouted back. "Nobody else would be mad enough to be abroad on such a day as this."

"Don't stand out there in the cold," Wake said. "We have a fire burning."

"I can see that," Tanner said, stepping into the small stand of trees. Even at a distance, he could feel the heat from the flames. The men's two horses were tethered on the far side of the clearing. "Clearly you do not fear we might have been followed."

Wake grinned.

"I thought if anyone should find us here, it would be you. If you'd been bested by the City Watch, they would have no reason to search for us out here. But if you'd beaten them, as I suspected you would, then the fire would be welcome after your travails and cold ride. Besides, it will be dark soon and we would not survive without fire on such a night. And as you said, who else would be foolish enough to brave this weather?" Wake looked behind Tanner, searching for the others. "Just you?" He was sitting with his back to the trunk of a tree, his voluminous cloak covering him completely. He shifted his position awkwardly, to peer into the grey-white landscape beyond Tanner.

"Raynald and Robert didn't make it," Tanner said.

Grim spat. Raising himself up to his full height with a grunt, he moved to the fire and poked at it with a stick.

"That is a pity," Wake said, sounding anything but sincere. "Though it might not be such a bad thing."

"Not a bad thing?" snarled Tanner. "Raynald and Rob were solid men. They died so that you could escape."

"They knew the risks," Wake said. "What of Dick and Roger? Did they meet their maker too?"

Tanner shook his head. Wake's callous dismissal of the men who had given their lives for him filled him with fury.

"They made it," he said, his tone gruff. "They're waiting back near the road. I wasn't sure what I was going to find here."

"Well, that is something, I suppose," said Wake. "These roads are dangerous, even with the likes of you and Grim with me. Dick and Roger make us into quite a formidable band. If we can offload the relic to the buyer at the agreed price, we should have enough to start afresh somewhere else. London perhaps. Or Bristol. We'll need all the money we can get."

Tanner had not wanted to confront Wake about the money that had been stolen from its hiding place. Not yet. But the man's sneering sent a roaring rage burning through him, searing away his caution in its savage heat.

"Well, you have more money now than is yours by right," he hissed, dropping his hand to the hilt of his sword.

"Come now, Hal," Wake said with a smile. "You are angry about the money you had stashed in the chimney of my tavern. But do not be angered. I have not stolen it. I merely took it for safekeeping. It is yours still, of course." He offered Tanner disarming smile. "Though I hope you might give me a loan, if I find myself in need."

Tanner stepped closer to the fire. Grimbald, sensing danger, moved away and picked up his huge club.

"You think I will believe any of your lies?" Tanner snapped. "You are a snake. You stole what was mine and if I had died along with Robert and Raynald, you would have been happy."

"You misunderstand me, Hal," Wake said. "You always did. You show great promise. You are quick-witted and tough. A good partner. I never wished you any ill." He flicked aside the cloak that covered his lap to reveal a crossbow. It was loaded with a vicious looking bolt. The point gleamed dully. It was aimed directly at Tanner. "But make no mistake, there comes a time when all partners become more of a hindrance than an asset."

Tanner did not move. Grim was only a couple of paces away, and Wake not much further than that. There was no way he could miss with the crossbow at such a short range. Tanner weighed up his chances. Whichever way he looked at it, he was going to die in the next few moments.

Then, shattering the tension like a skein of ice on a puddle, from the distance came a shouted voice. Confused, Tanner turned towards the voice that was calling his name.

He did not notice Wake rising smoothly to his feet, taking advantage of this new distraction to lift his crossbow and take aim.

CHAPTER SIXTEEN

"Look, you fucking oaf, if you don't let us out of here, I'm going to lose my temper!"

The sergeant at Walmgate Barre blanched at John's threat, but he raised an eyebrow at the massive bailiff atop his horse and replied, "Only then?"

"Trust me," Tuck told the man dryly. "That's calm for him. You really don't want to see Little John when he's lost his temper."

Again, the sergeant seemed to pale, his face blending in with the falling snow so white did he become. "Little John?"

"Aye! Have you heard of him?" It was Ivor who spoke up now. "We came here from Leeds with John and Tuck on the king's business – hunting men who attacked a priest in Pontefract and ransacked the place, stealing a priceless relic and murdering members of the hue and cry who tried to stop them escaping."

The gate guard's mouth opened and he stared at the men he'd detained.

"The men we're after – William Wake, Hal Tanner, and a giant named Grimbald de Pendok – escaped through these gates a short time ago." John nudged his horse forward, nodding at the barred gates that were holding up their pursuit of the fugitives. "You must have seen them. In fact, I'm guessing they paid you to delay us so they could make good their escape."

"What? No. We just need to search you and make sure you are who you say you are before we let you leave, it's perfectly routine. I'd never—"

John spoke over him loudly, not interested in his excuses. "Those men have murdered at least six of your comrades, did you know that? Aye, in the Black Swan. There's a man tied to a chair upstairs, looks like he was tortured and then stabbed to death. His cries must have brought the City Watch and Wake and his lackeys fought them off, killing every last one!"

This revelation brought outrage from the other gate guards, as John had expected.

"Now, as you've been told, we're on the king's official business, hunting murderers. Are you going to stand in our way, or move aside and let us be about our task?" He hefted his quarterstaff and bared his teeth like a great wolf. "I'm warning you though, if you don't get out of my way, you won't live to see the morning with all your limbs intact."

Behind the sergeant the guards had already put away their weapons and now hurried to the gates, dragging the heavy locking bars clear and opening the way for John and his companions to leave the city.

"I know you took a bribe from Wake or Tanner," John growled at the sergeant, climbing back onto his horse and tucking his staff under his arm. "If the bastards escape because of that, well, you'd better leave the city yourself, for I'll be back to find you, and whatever they paid won't be worth the kicking you'll get."

"Do you know where they're going?" Tuck asked as his horse trotted past the sergeant. "If so, tell us and go some way to redeeming yourself."

The sergeant looked down at the slush-filled road and one of the other gate guards cried, "Tell them, if you know! The bastards have killed our friends – Wake and Tanner are outlaws now, they're not going to be back in York anytime soon."

"Fine!" the guard sighed, throwing up his hands, utterly defeated. "Wake left a while ago, with Grimbald. Tanner and his mates went out some time later. I heard one of them saying they were going to Brough first, before riding on to Ravenser Odd."

John was through the gates by now but he heard the sergeant and turned back to look at Tuck. "Brough. That's a good thirty miles from here, and the snow still hasn't let up."

"Then we better get moving," the friar called, pulling up his hood and huddling down as the six horsemen moved out of York and began riding to the southeast.

* * *

The horses had not been ridden that hard over the past few days, but the animals did not find it easy moving in mud, frost, and snow. John knew how tired his muscles were after some time spent walking in such terrain, where one had to take care with every step, so he felt sorry for their mounts as they tried to reach Brough as quickly as possible. It wasn't just physically exhausting trotting in the midst of December, it took a toll mentally as well, especially when the snow continued to fall, turning the world into a strange, drifting mass of white that made one's eyes ache or even see things that weren't there.

Despite all this, thirty miles was not a great distance, especially since the road was fairly level, cutting south and avoiding the hills to the east. The riders stopped twice to allow the animals to rest, and everyone in the party had some food and water. There was little talk for the weather was oppressive and besides, what was there to talk about? The six men knew they would face a desperate fight if they caught up with Wake and Tanner.

How many lackeys did the fugitives have with them? How many had escaped from the Black Swan and headed to Brough? John had no qualms over fighting beside Friar Tuck, but the others were an unknown quantity. Ivor and his men spoke well, and carried themselves confidently, but whether they'd actually be any use against the likes of the giant Grim remained to be seen.

John wished he had more information on the men they hunted. All he really knew was that William Wake was a vicious gang leader it was best not to upset, Hal Tanner acted as some kind of enforcer for Wake, and Grim was well named. John glanced down, making sure his longbow was still attached to his saddle, and his string was well protected from the damp within the pouch he carried inside his woollen cloak. It would be best if they could face the outlaws from a distance, catching them unawares and whittling down their numbers with well-aimed arrows.

Murmuring reached John in the depressing stillness and he glanced to his right, seeing Tuck, a thin shroud of pale, white snow coating him as his mittened fingers grasped his pectoral cross and he prayed to Christ for the success of their mission. The bailiff smiled – it was good to have such a friend at one's side. Not merely a warrior, but a man who had God and His angels onside. John doubted if Wake and Tanner were on good terms with God, given their crimes and the heinous attack on the church in Pontefract.

Still, it was not always holy men who proved victorious, and John was well aware that their enemies must be approached with caution.

"Look!" It was Ivor who'd called out in a low voice, then repeated himself when his shout was lost in the falling snow.

John glanced around and saw Ivor pointing excitedly off to the left, where the land sloped downwards between some trees, seemingly towards a dale or dell.

"What is it?" Tuck asked, red-faced as he pushed back his hood, apparently too hot despite the frigid air.

"Look," said Ivor and his three comrades from Leeds joined in, also pointing at the snowy ground. One of them even dismounted and knelt to examine what John now realised were fresh tracks.

"They must have been left recently," said the man who'd knelt for a closer look. "Or the snow would have covered them completely." He scanned the prints, walking down the slope a short distance before hurrying back to report his findings. "I'd say at least five horses, possibly more."

"It has to be the men we're after," Ivor said, eyes shining as he fingered the sword at his waist. "We must be close."

John wondered what they should do. Perhaps he should scout ahead – it wouldn't do any good to simply stumble into the backs of the fugitives and remove any element of surprise. Then again, the outlaws wouldn't be expecting pursuit this soon – John and his riders had moved far quicker than York's militia would, and the gate sergeant had also told them exactly where Wake and Tanner were heading.

"Come on," the bailiff said, urging his horse to the front of the formation. He would not expect anyone else to take point and face possible danger first. "Stay alert, they can't be too far ahead."

The horses picked their way down the slope carefully. Thankfully it was not too steep, but the snow made it treacherous, and it took what felt like an age before all six riders were on level ground again, moving in single file which also made John feel terribly exposed.

The snow had let up if just for a short time, allowing a better view of the terrain and, not too far ahead, a plume of grey smoke curled languidly into the sky.

John held up a hand and drew his horse to a stop. The rest of the group saw the smoke now and followed John's lead as he dismounted, pointing to the left where the track widened into a copse of twisted, leafless trees.

"We'll leave our mounts tethered there," the towering bailiff called softly back to his men as he led the way. "Make sure you take all your weapons, longbows, arrows and anything else you need before we leave the animals. Hit them from a distance, if you can, with your arrows."

No one spoke. No discussion over what the smoke might signify. It was obvious: they had reached the end of their road, and the men they'd followed from Pontefract lay just ahead, so confident they were safe that they'd made a fire. John pictured the arrogant bastards sitting around the merry blaze, warm and content with skins of ale and mouths full of salted beef.

Well, they'd get a shock soon enough, and the Virgin of the Mountains would soon be making its way back to All Saints' where it would heal the dying child.

John checked his sword was securely buckled in place then he tied his horse to a sapling before unclipping his staff and stringing his longbow. He turned to watch the others make their own preparations. All appeared confident, if a little anxious, which was entirely natural. Even John had butterflies in his belly as he looked again at the smoke rising into the grey sky perhaps a quarter of a mile ahead.

"Ready?" he rumbled, moving from man to man before finally reaching Tuck, who nodded grimly.

"Let's deal with these evil bastards," said the friar. "And then have a rest at their fire, for it's bloody freezing!"

Grinning, John clapped him on the shoulder and moved forwards, doing his best to crouch as he walked, although even then he was still huge. He gestured with two fingers to his left, and then to his right, and the soldiers from Leeds split up as ordered, flanking John and Tuck as they crept ahead.

Voices could be heard ahead and now the unmistakable scent of roasting meat drifted on the wintry air. John slowed and Tuck followed suit. To their left, their two companions slipped between the trees, keeping pace with them, while the two on the right moved slightly ahead, using the evergreen needles of a handy juniper bush as cover.

"There they are!" Tuck hissed, raising his longbow and aiming it towards the rising smoke where the shape of a prodigiously tall man could now be seen standing.

John raised his own bow and nocked an arrow to the string, feeling the battle fever begin to pound in his veins, pins and needles running along his arms until, just a heartbeat later, calm fell upon him and he took aim at the giant figure that must be Grimbald.

"Wait until we see another one," Tuck murmured. "Might as well take two out at the same time, and make this easier for ourselves."

They did see someone else just at that moment, as a second man stood before the fire, hands outstretched as though warming himself.

"Hal!"

John turned in horror to see Ivor standing, waving towards the fugitives' camp.

"Hal! It's me, Ivor. We fought together in the war! Your mates murdered some guards back in York, and we're here to arrest them. Get yourself to safety, friend!"

"What the hell is he doing?" John hissed, enraged to have lost the element of surprise. "He'll get us all killed. Shut him up, Tuck!"

The friar nodded and hurried through the trees towards Ivor, hissing at the man to be silent.

Just before Tuck reached the man, the twang of a crossbow reverberated around the woods and, a moment later, there came a thud and a scream of agony. Ivor stood, back arched in agony, eyes bulging, a crossbow bolt in the side of his neck. As John watched, a second projectile, this time a long, white-fletched arrow, tore through the air and struck Ivor directly in the face, the man's head erupting in an explosion of gore before he fell out of sight.

"It's a trap," John said, mind whirling as his voice rose in a great warning bellow, desperately trying to save the others from Ivor's terrible fate. "It's a trap! It's a fucking trap, by Christ! Fall back!"

CHAPTER SEVENTEEN

Tanner's mind reeled. One instant he had been facing certain death at the hands of Grimbald and Wake, the next his name was being shouted by a voice he had not heard in years. It took him a moment to place the owner of the voice, but recognition came all at once as he spied the man standing on the path.

"Ivor?" Tanner called out. "Is that you?"

Before his erstwhile brother-in-arms could reply, Wake's crossbow discharged with a loud slapping sound. Tanner flinched, but the bolt had not been meant for him. Ivor grunted, clawing the stubby bolt that jutted from his neck.

"What have you done?" Tanner hissed at Wake.

"Evened the odds," Wake said, flinging himself behind one of the trees and pulling another bolt from a bag that hung from his belt.

Tanner was still trying to make sense of what was happening. There were more men out there, their shapes diffuse and shadowy in the snowstorm and gathering twilight. Tanner had known all the men of the Watch in York and he was sure Ivor had not been one of them. But there was no doubt Ivor was there now, seriously wounded by Wake.

These men had come for those who had killed the watchmen in York. How Ivor came to be among them and how they were able to be so quickly on their trail Tanner had no idea, but he owed the man something for the warning he had given.

Taking in a deep breath, Tanner was about to shout his own warning, knowing it might well be too late to save his old friend. But before he could utter another sound, he heard the thwack of a bowstring and an arrow slammed into Ivor's face, knocking him from his feet in a spray of blood. The arrow had come from the side, from the wall and the snow-blanketed holly tree.

Roger! Tanner knew Dick was no archer, but Roger and his brother had both trained at the butts all their lives and they both took pride in their abilities with the longbow. There would be no surviving an arrow from Roger's bow from that distance.

One of the men near Ivor was huge, as tall as Grim perhaps. He started bellowing orders at the others and they separated, darting for whatever cover they could find. But not before the giant loosed an arrow of his own. Tanner ducked instinctively and the arrow slammed into the nearest alder, the fletchings quivering no more than a hand's breadth from his face.

Tanner flung himself behind the tree as another arrow fizzed over his head to be lost in the snowy gloaming. Behind a nearby tree, Wake was spanning his crossbow and placing a fresh bolt ready to shoot.

For a short while there was no movement. The only sounds were the wind whispering through the icy branches of the alders, the nervous stamping of the horses that Grim and Wake had tethered under the trees, and the panting breath of the men cowering behind the protection of the trunks.

A booming voice, as loud as thunder came to them then from behind the scant shelter of a juniper bush.

"I am John Little, Bailiff of Sir Henry de Faucumberg, the Sheriff of Nottingham and Yorkshire. We've come to bring you men to justice for your crimes, and to return the relic you stole to its rightful place. No doubt you've heard of me, William Wake. You have nowhere to run. Give yourselves up now and I'll see that you're treated fairly."

Wake leaned out from his hiding place and snapped off another shot, aiming at John's voice. Without waiting to see if he had struck any of their assailants, he dropped back behind the tree and placed his foot in the crossbow's stirrup, pulling the string taut again. He shouted as he went about reloading his weapon.

"I've heard of you alright, Little John!" he yelled. "Got yourself a noble patron, have you? I don't believe for a moment you have changed that much from when you were a wolf's head. There are enough of us to fight. I'm not about to give up the Virgin of the Mountains just so you can sell it yourself!"

Wake finished spanning and reloading his crossbow and nodded to Grimbald, who had so far not moved. Tanner, the fire warm on his face, watched as the giant slipped between the trees and vanished from sight. Tanner had seen the man fight many times, but had never seen him move with such careful grace. Despite his size, he moved as silently as a wraith.

A different voice now shouted from the cold.

"We are not wolf's heads. My name is Tuck. I'm a friar, a servant of God, and I have vowed to take the holy relic back to Pontefract. There's a child there who has need of its powers."

"Powers you say?" Wake's voice dripped with scorn. "Surely you do not believe in such old wives' tales. Next you will be telling me that the bones sold by Pardoners are actually the bones of Christ Himself and not fished out of a pork stew."

"God is great," shouted Tuck, "and His power is boundless. A man in your position should not turn away from the Lord, for He can work miracles, and He can forgive even a sinner such as you."

Wake let out a harsh laugh.

"It would be a miracle indeed if God forgave my sins."

Tanner watched Wake, aghast at the man's blaspheming. He had himself long since given up believing in the goodness of God, but he had never dared voice his opinions out loud. To hear Wake do so now, and to a man of the cloth no less, made Tanner's skin crawl.

Seeing Tanner's shocked expression, Wake winked at him and grinned.

"You spoke of a child," he shouted. "What need has a child for an old relic?"

"The relic has cured many sick people. There's a girl in Pontefract. She's terribly ill and will surely die without the Virgin's intervention."

Tanner ground his teeth. Where had God been when May was sick? There had been no relic to save his daughter. Unbidden, the memory of her tiny shroud being lowered into the earth filled his mind's eye. Without knowing he was going to speak, Tanner found himself suddenly shouting.

"Lies!" he yelled, his anger making his voice crack. "What does God care? He cares naught whether children live or die."

Wake was nodding.

"That's good," he whispered. "Keep them talking."

Tanner frowned, realising he had never told Wake of May's death. He had never spoken of her to anyone in York. Her death was his secret pain, to be borne alone. He felt ashamed of his outburst now, even as the friar called back to him, his voice thin and strained.

"You're wrong," Tuck said. "God is love. We cannot say why He chooses to allow some to live and others to die, but who are we to question His ways? Know this, the girl in Pontefract is waiting for the Virgin of the Mountains, and we've sworn to bring it to her. God is on our side, and we *will* prevail against you."

Wake glanced around the tree, and grinned at what he saw. Tanner followed his gaze, but could make out little in the blizzard of snowflakes.

"You say God is on your side," shouted Wake.

"He is, and you would do well not to forget it."

"I'll take my chances," Wake replied, his tone strangely gleeful, "for Grim is on ours!"

And with that, the huge shape of Grimbald de Pendok surged up from where he had crept through the snow, hidden by bushes, trees and rocks. He threw himself at Little John, who parried a crushing blow from Grim's cudgel, and then leapt into the fray swinging his stout staff as if it weighed no more than a twig. The two massive men spun away, their weapons clacking as they fought.

Shocked by the sudden appearance of the club-wielding giant, two of the guards who had been cowering out of sight now leapt up and made to flee back to their horses. Roger's bowstring twanged and the first fell into the snow, an arrow between his shoulder blades. The second one didn't make it much further before another arrow pierced his neck, dark blood spurting into the carpet of snow.

The dusk was full of movement, snow falling thickly on the fighting men. Tanner fancied he saw Roger and the smaller figure of Richard Blount too, rushing towards the Sheriff's men, but it was hard to make out what was happening in any detail.

One thing he did see was the form of Friar Tuck moving to his comrades' defence. For an instant, the tonsured man was clearly visible in the middle of the path. Beside Tanner, Wake stepped out from behind the tree, aiming his crossbow at the friar. He paused for a heartbeat, adjusting his aim, then pulled the lever, sending the deadly bolt flying into the blizzard.

CHAPTER EIGHTEEN

Wake had already proven he was a good shot with his crossbow, and his bolt would surely have struck the friar, if Tanner had not knocked the weapon aside at the instant Wake pulled the trigger lever. Caught by surprise, Wake dropped the crossbow with a clatter into the muddy snow. The bolt vanished in the gathering gloom, whizzing harmlessly over the heads of the friar and the others fighting on the path. Tanner was vaguely aware of the hulking shapes of Grim and John locked in battle, their grunts and the clack of their weapons loud in the unnatural stillness of the snow-wreathed land.

But he could not look for long enough to see who had the upper hand, for Wake, though initially off-guard, had the reflexes of a cornered rat and had produced a wicked-looking knife.

The mention of the sickly girl had flooded Tanner's mind with darkness and fury, pulling him away from thoughts of how he might save himself from his current predicament. Tuck's words had the ring of truth about them. Tanner knew not whether the relic had any power to heal the sick, but the friar certainly believed. When Tanner saw Wake about to kill the holy man without remorse, like a bowstring pulled too far, something had snapped within him.

"You think they'll forgive you, if you kill me?" Wake scoffed. "Think they'll just allow you to leave here?" He slashed at Tanner, hoping to catch him unprepared. Tanner leapt back, drawing his sword.

Wake's blade flickered a hand's breadth from his face.

"I don't think we'll leave here with our lives, but I would rather kill you than see you hang," Tanner replied. "You were going to murder me if we got out of here anyway."

"Of course I was!" hissed Wake, circling around to his right, wary of Tanner's longer blade. "You've gone soft, Hal. You're no use to me now."

Without warning, Wake lunged. Tanner was ready and easily parried Wake's blade. He smiled, but at the same instant, he felt a pressure in his side.

Pulling away, he looked down. There was blood on his tunic. On seeing this, pain bloomed in his side, just below his ribs.

Wake sneered and Tanner saw how mistaken he had been in his complacency. Wake held in his left hand the small blade he had used to cut Laurence's throat. Tanner had not seen him produce the second knife. Silently cursing his stupidity, Tanner stamped forward, swinging his sword. He could not afford to underestimate Wake again.

Tanner had never watched Wake fight before. The older man preferred to leave violence to his lackeys, but now Tanner saw William Wake was no stranger to combat. Keeping his balance on the balls of his feet, Wake skipped away from Tanner's scything sword. Tanner could feel his blood soaking his shirt and the waistband of his hose. In the distance he could still hear the sounds of fighting. He would have to finish this quickly.

He attacked again.

Once more, Wake danced out of reach, leading him past the blazing fire and further into the trees. Tanner lunged. Wake jumped back, pushing the blade away with his dagger. Tanner gritted his teeth. He had the longer blade, and if Wake stood his ground, the fight would be over in moments. But Wake knew this. And with every passing heartbeat, Tanner was weakening from his wound. Wake grinned savagely, content to evade his attacks a while longer. Until Tanner tired, or...

With a horrifying sense of foreboding, Tanner leapt back. He was suddenly certain he knew why Wake was stalling. Distancing himself from Wake, Tanner risked a look over his shoulder.

Tanner sighed. There, beside the fire stood Dick. He had somehow managed to extricate himself from the fight with the Sheriff's men and now he held Wake's crossbow. He must have found bolts beside the tree too, for the weapon was spanned and loaded. The gleaming tip of the bolt was aimed directly at Tanner.

"Do it!" said Wake.

Dick hesitated, his eyes flicked between Tanner and Wake. Tanner seized on the opportunity.

"You're not a killer, Dick," he said. "You never were."

Dick licked his lips nervously. The crossbow wavered.

"Shoot him, Dick," Wake said. "There is no time to waste."

"He's right," said Tanner. "There is no time. It is too late for Wake and me. You heard the Sheriff's men, they know our names. But you can still run.

Take one of the horses and go. If you stay, you'll hang for what you've done. Or I'll kill you myself."

"Not if I kill you," Dick said, defiantly raising the crossbow.

"Yes," hissed Wake, "kill him. Now!"

Tanner shook his head.

"You're not going to kill me, Dick," Tanner said. He had not taken his eyes off the youth as they spoke, but he was aware of Wake moving stealthily away from him, distancing himself in case Dick should miss his target.

Taking a deep breath, Tanner began to stride purposefully towards Dick.

"Give me the bow," he said, holding out his hand. "Give it to me and run while you still have time. You're young. You can still make a life for yourself. Ride away."

"Don't you dare," hissed Wake. "You fucking coward!"

Dick bit his lip. His eyes flicked from one of them to the other. Then, mind made up, he dropped the crossbow at his feet and darted away towards the horses.

Tanner didn't hesitate. Sweeping up the crossbow, he spun and pulled the lever. The bolt did not strike Wake in the chest as he had hoped, instead it scored a deep cut across his left thigh.

Out of Tanner's line of sight, he heard a horse whinny, then the thrum of hooves as it galloped away. Perhaps Dick would escape, Tanner thought. If he survived this, which looked doubtful, he wouldn't go looking for the boy. He'd meant what he'd said. He had never much liked the lad, but Dick was little more than a child who had made bad decisions. Perhaps he was young enough that he could pull himself out of the dark world he'd inhabited and start a new life. Tanner had given him that chance. It was up to Richard Blount what he did with it.

Wake cursed and hobbled away, perhaps hoping to reach the other horse tied at the edge of the clearing. Tossing the crossbow aside, Tanner sprang after him. He was growing weak now, but he caught up with Wake in moments.

Wake turned to face him, both knives raised. But he was slower now, and Tanner was in no mood to listen to his taunts. He slashed at Wake, who parried the blow on his dagger. Tanner caught his left wrist in an iron grip, twisting the limb so that the bloody knife fell from Wake's hand. Then, pulling Wake towards him, Tanner smashed his forehead into his nose. Cartilage crunched. Blood sprayed. Wake sagged and staggered back. Then, with a snarl like an animal, he launched himself at Tanner once more.

Tanner sidestepped the headlong rush and drove his sword between Wake's ribs. Wake's eyes widened in shock and agony.

"I should have killed you when I had the chance," he said, his voice wheezing, blood bubbling on his lips.

"Still think I've gone soft?" whispered Tanner.

Wake didn't reply. His eyes stared unseeing at Tanner. Dragging his sword free, Tanner shoved Wake's corpse away. Finally allowing his weariness to overcome him, he fell to his knees beside his former partner.

The ground was so cold, the snow falling heavier than ever. Tanner began to tremble. He could hear nothing now save for the rush of his blood in his ears, the crackle of the fire and the wind whistling through the trees.

A footfall crunching in the snow alerted him to someone's approach.

"Tanner?" a gruff voice said.

With a sigh, Henry Tanner pushed himself to his feet and turned around slowly, sword in hand and ready to fight one last time.

CHAPTER NINETEEN

Friar Tuck stood on the far edge of the woods trying to reason with the outlaws they'd been hunting. A short distance away, John watched, crouching behind a low bush, wary of more crossbow bolts or arrows coming from the outlaw camp ahead, so it was a shock when he heard a crunch in the snow behind him. Turning, he found himself face to face with a giant intent on crushing his skull. He knew it was Grimbald de Pendok, and Little John could not remember ever meeting a man not only as tall as he was, but also as broad.

Desperately, the bailiff brought up his quarterstaff, just managing to knock aside the heavy cudgel that would certainly have killed him had it landed.

"Little John, eh?" Grim demanded, lip curling as he rolled his shoulders almost like a rutting stag displaying its strength. "You don't look that big to me." He swung his cudgel again, aiming this time for John's elbow.

Dancing back away from the attack, Little John struck out with his own great weapon. "Bigger than you, Grim, you ugly twat," he grunted, feeling his staff knocked aside with tremendous force and trying to balance himself as the snow shifted, becoming icy and slippery beneath the combatants.

"I'm not so sure about that," Grim retorted, launching another flurry of attacks, cudgel whipping through the frigid air with blinding speed. "I'll measure you when you're dead and laid out flat in the snow!"

John was stunned by the speed of his opponent's movements. Grim's feet seemed to find purchase on the slippery ground far better than John could manage, and the bailiff was pushed backwards, teeth gritted as he swung his quarterstaff faster and faster, unable to launch an attack of his own as the cudgel hammered against him, seeking for an opening. John knew that even a glancing blow from that dull weapon could shatter his bones and leave him completely incapacitated, and he shook his long hair away from his eyes, brow coated in sweat despite the cold.

Forced back through the blizzard, squinting, constantly on the back foot, unable to bring the greater reach of his staff to bear, John felt a seed of fear begin to grow and blossom within his guts. Grimbald's strikes were relentless, and it was only a matter of time before one made it past John's defences.

Two of the remaining guards that had travelled with them from Leeds broke free of the trees they'd sought cover behind and ran away, towards the horses. John could see the men in his peripheral vision, slipping and falling, pushing themselves up and struggling through the deep snow. The sound of a longbow filled the air and an arrow took one of the fleeing guards in the back.

"You're losing this fight," Grim laughed, reaching out and grabbing John's staff with his left hand. "Your men are dying, and so will you, lawman."

John wrenched his staff free, momentarily knocking his huge enemy off balance. Taking a chance, the bailiff kicked out, catching Grim on the side of the knee. It rocked his foe but did not bring him down. The outlaw's mocking smile disappeared though, replaced by a murderous frown.

"That the best you've got?" Grim hissed, moving forward, as relentless and unstoppable as the sea, or the falling snow. "Thought you were some legendary hero."

John felt his feet suddenly gain purchase, and realised he'd been forced beneath a thick stand of trees. The snow was not so thick on the ground here and he was able to finally set himself in a strong, defensive stance. Grim continued to come after him but, behind the massive outlaw, John saw the second of the fleeing guardsmen from Leeds cut down by another arrow, the fellow sprawling on the ground, arms and legs outstretched in the thick, white blanket.

"No!" the bailiff cried in despair.

Grimbald took advantage of John's distress, forgoing his cudgel for once, and instead lashing out with a kick of his own, catching the bailiff in the stomach. As John fell backwards against one of the trees, the cudgel swung around again, smashing against the side of John's forehead.

Stars exploded in his vision but he knew he was dead if he went down. Snarling like a dog, the bailiff dropped his quarterstaff and threw himself at Grim, hands grasping his opponent around the throat, squeezing with every ounce of strength he could muster.

Grimbald tried to break the bailiff's grip, but they'd moved back onto the snow and the footing was treacherous. As John pushed, Grim's feet gave way and the combatants fell over.

Somehow, John found himself on his back, underneath the enormous weight of Grimbald de Pendok. The bailiff had lost his grip on the enemy's throat, and the roles were suddenly reversed.

"Thought you'd choke me to death, you bastard?" Grim roared, massive, meaty hands squeezing John's neck, thumbs pressing viciously into his windpipe, crushing him down into the snow. "See how you like it, lawman!"

John's mouth opened, but he could not speak, could not breathe as his tongue seemed to swell, filling his mouth and throat. Panic swept through him and he struggled desperately to break Grim's hold, but the outlaw was unbelievably strong, and John felt his strength fading along with his consciousness.

"Hurry up and die," Grim shouted, spittle flying, eyes bulging as he pressed down harder and harder, joyous as he murdered another man. "Die, Little John, and then I'll find your friend, Tuck, and end him too."

John tried to scream but only a tortured gasp came out as he lifted his hands to Grim's face, almost caressing the savage outlaw who seemed to take pleasure in the sensation, grin widening viciously.

And then Little John's thumbs were over Grim's eyes and, with one last, desperate surge of strength, the bailiff pressed hard into the soft, white orbs.

The weight fell away from John as Grim reeled back, screaming incoherently, hands covering his eyes as he stood up and flailed around like a madman with no purpose or understanding of what was happening.

Gasping and wheezing, Little John's fingers scrabbled in the snow, finding at last his quarterstaff and drawing it to him like a lover. He pushed himself to his feet and used the staff to keep him there as he drew in deep, burning breaths. Grim continued to cry and wail, cursing John and threatening to tear the bailiff apart with his bare hands.

John waited until he was able to stand without the aid of his staff, nausea receding, stars slowly fading from his vision, and then he raised his weapon.

"Where are you, you bastard?" Grimbald screeched. "I'll fucking kill you for this! You've blinded me!"

"I'm here," John replied coldly, and swung the quarterstaff through the falling white flakes in a wide arc. The massive length of ash cannoned against Grim's head and the outlaw was thrown to the side, falling into the snow like a sack of carrots. It had been a killing blow, of that there could be no doubt.

Letting out a long sigh, John lowered his staff and placed his weight on it once more, staring at the man lying on the clean, white ground, a ruined, viscous mess where his eyes had been.

The battle was far from over however, and a shout of alarm from Tuck brought John back to reality. He turned and saw the last of the guards that had come with them from Leeds grappling with another outlaw. For some reason the guard was not armed, and the outlaw was fending him off with a longbow.

John started towards them but he was so exhausted from his titanic fight with Grimbald that he could barely move, feet dragging infuriatingly on the frigid ground. As he watched, the outlaw swung his bow, catching the guard a savage blow beneath the chin.

Tuck was racing towards them as fast as he could in the terrible conditions, but he was too far away to stop the outlaw smashing his bow down again and again on the fallen guard.

"In the name of God, stop!"

The outlaw looked up, face splattered with blood, and blanched at the sight of the burly friar charging towards him, sword in hand. The longbow was dropped, snapped in two from smashing the poor guard to death, and a sword drawn in its stead.

"Look out, Tuck!" John cried. "I'm coming!"

The friar did not wait, racing straight for the outlaw who thrust his sword towards him.

John forced himself to jog through the thick, powdery snow, legs aching, praying that God would help his friend against the bowman who'd already killed three of the men from Leeds.

Tuck was a Franciscan friar, a man of God who sought to carry peace and love wherever he went. But he was also a warrior, and, before John could reach the two combatants, Tuck had parried every attack the outlaw could throw at him before neatly stepping inside a wild thrust and plunging the point of his sword deep into the enemy's guts.

"May Christ have mercy on your soul," Tuck murmured sadly, withdrawing his blade and cleaning it on the dying outlaw's cloak before wiping it through the snow to make sure every crimson drop was erased from the steel.

"Are you alright?" John asked, coming to stand beside his friend and placing a massive arm around the friar's shoulders.

Tuck turned to look at him and raised his eyebrows at what he saw. "I should be asking you that question," he said. "You're in a right state. There's a lump the size of a hen's egg on your forehead."

John laughed but it caught in his damaged throat and a coughing fit overtook him. Tuck patted him on the back until it passed, and then, grinning, John said, "You think I'm a mess? You should see the state of the bastard I was fighting!"

"Well, the poor fellows from Leeds are all dead," Tuck told him sorrowfully. "But there's still outlaws alive, and we still haven't found the relic. Come on, we have to finish this."

John nodded and drew himself up straight, forcing himself to ignore the pain and exhaustion that filled every part of his being. He followed the friar through the trees, warily moving from trunk to trunk in case more of those damned arrows or crossbow bolts were loosed in their direction.

"Look, there!" Tuck hissed, pointing off to the right.

The blizzard had not let up, but they could see a man on horseback disappearing into the dense white flakes, evidently making his escape.

"That's one less to worry about," John noted.

"Well, let's hope he's not got the relic or we might never find it," Tuck said bleakly. "But look, there's another two of the Godless fools there."

John followed him again as they pushed on through the snow, and the trees which gave way to a clearing.

"That's Tanner," Tuck said as they drew closer to a man kneeling over another in the snow.

"And that must be Wake on the ground," the bailiff breathed, seeing then that the second man was dead.

They walked on, closing the gap between them and the single remaining outlaw.

"Tanner!" John called when they were just a few yards away.

The man turned to look at them and, with an air of resignation, he rose and set his feet, sword raised, ready to defend himself to the death.

"Where's the relic, Tanner?" John asked.

The outlaw shrugged. "I don't know. I don't have it, Wake did."

"There's been enough death here today," Tuck stated. "All we want is that relic, and you can go on your way."

Tanner laughed in disbelief. "You would just let me go?" he demanded. "Just like that? After everything that's happened here?"

John nodded. "I saw you pushing Wake aside when he was taking aim at the friar. If it wasn't for you, Tuck would be dead. I'd say that counts for something. Just give us the statuette, Tanner."

"You said there was a girl that might be saved by its power."

John nodded. "That's why we're here."

Tanner eyed the bailiff suspiciously before turning his gaze on Tuck and, at last, his shoulders slumped and he lowered his sword. "I wasn't lying. I don't have the relic." He kicked the body at his feet. "Wake here had it. You're welcome to search his flea-bitten corpse for it."

John and Tuck moved forward as Tanner stepped back warily. The friar bent, quickly going through Wake's garments but coming up empty-handed. "Nothing," he sighed.

"Well, I'm certain he had it before you found us," Tanner told them firmly. "So it must be here somewhere."

"What about the boy that rode off?"

"Dick? No chance Wake would have given it to him. No, it must be nearby."

John and Tuck looked about, and the bailiff shook his head in despair. "We'll never find it in this blizzard. It could be anywhere, buried under a foot of snow!"

"And by the time it melts, it'll be too late to help that little girl," Tuck added in frustration.

The three men stood in silence, all sound swallowed up by the blizzard so it was as if they were alone on an island in an ocean of white.

"Wait," Tanner said at last, shaking his head, brow furrowed. "I almost forgot, it feels like it happened so long ago. Wake stashed something just before I walked into the camp, when he didn't know I was watching him." He swung around and began forcing his way through the snow towards the remains of an old drystone wall. Much of it had collapsed some time ago, and a pile of lichen encrusted stones lay behind what was left of it.

John and Tuck followed the outlaw, still wary and unwilling to trust this man who was a renowned killer. For his part, Tanner seemed to have forgotten all about them and the danger they posed, as he leaned down and began digging in the snow with his gloved hands, shifting the fallen stones, tossing them aside, utterly intent on his task.

It did not take long.

"Here!" he cried, raising leather saddlebags and holding them up triumphantly. "The relic has to be in here."

John felt his heart begin to race again as Tanner removed his gloves and, fingers numb from the cold, struggled for what felt like an age with the buckle that held the sack closed. At last, the clasp was undone, and the top of the bag was drawn open.

"Is that it?" John demanded breathlessly, terrified the hope that had suddenly risen within him would be dashed. "Is that the Virgin of the Mountains?"

"It's valuable this, isn't it?" Tanner asked as he drew out something wrapped in a piece of linen. "Priceless, almost."

Tuck laid a hand on John's arm as the furious bailiff opened his mouth to reply. "It is," the friar admitted. "That's why your acquaintance, Wake, wanted it. But what does silver matter when compared to the life of a child, Tanner?"

To John's amazement, tears filled Tanner's eyes, and the man turned away from them, angrily wiping his face. For a long time no one said anything, and then, at last, the outlaw looked at them again, and held out the linen-shrouded relic. "Here," he said gruffly. "If it can save the little girl's life, you should take it to her."

John stepped forward warily, half expecting Tanner to drop the saddlebags and attack him, but the relic was handed over and the two parties stepped back again, a safe distance between them as the linen was unwrapped and Tuck confirmed that this was, indeed, the Virgin of the Mountains.

The quest for the wooden statuette had taken a heavy toll, but they had retrieved it at last.

"Thank you," said John.

"And thank you again," Tuck added. "For saving my life."

Tanner nodded. There were no tears in his eyes now and John wondered if it had merely been snow melting on his face for the outlaw was smiling and seemed quite at peace with the way things had turned out. "Where's Grim?" he asked then.

"Dead," John replied. "I killed him."

Tanner chuckled darkly. "Good."

"What will you do now?" Tuck asked him.

"Now? I reckon I will probably just sit and try to get the fire going again." He looked down and gingerly touched his side, just below his ribs which, John saw now, was slick with blood.

"He's injured, Tuck." The massive bailiff sheathed his sword and moved to grasp Tanner under the arms, all thoughts of fighting now gone. "Come on, let's get him over to their campfire." Between them, they helped him over to the outlaws' campsite, and John brought the fire roaring back to life, bringing one of the tents over and placing it around Tuck as the friar ordered Tanner to strip off his cloak and gambeson.

"But it's bloody freezing!" the outlaw protested.

"And you'll be bloody dead if we don't get that looked at. John, run back to our horses and bring my pack, eh? It's got my medical supplies in it."

John hesitated, staring at Tanner, wondering if the man could be trusted not to attack Tuck and steal back the precious relic. There was no duplicity in the outlaw's eyes though, and the bailiff did as he was told, returning soon after with the bandages and other supplies.

No one spoke as the friar cleaned the wound, stitched it shut, and wound a bandage around his torso. It was not an awkward silence, but there was a distinct feeling of sadness over the camp as the snow finally stopped and night fell.

Tanner thanked Tuck for tending to his wound and then they shared some meat that John heated over the fire. There was ale in the camp too, and plenty of it, which made the icy night somewhat more enjoyable as the freezing moon crept up and watched over them. The horses were brought closer, and it wasn't long before the three men, utterly spent after their deadly exertions, were fast asleep.

When John awoke the next day the sun was up, and the air was crisp, and clean, and fresh. Tuck woke soon after and they broke their fast on bread and cheese.

Of Tanner there was no sign.

"We ready to move then?" Friar Tuck asked, tearing down the camp and packing everything they could on the horses. They had extra now, since they had the dead men's animals and equipment, but it did not take them long to gather it all together.

"Aye, I'm ready," John said. "Hopefully the road isn't too bad. Come on, old friend, let's finish this and get back to Wakefield."

CHAPTER TWENTY

Little John and Tuck did not ride directly back to Pontefract with the holy relic. First, they made for Leeds, with the bodies of Ivor and the other three guards strapped to their horses. There, John signed a note for the bailiff, Edmund Vessey to send to Sheriff de Faucumberg, outlining the part the four brave men had played in putting an end to Wake and his gang, and retrieving the priceless Virgin of the Mountains.

"The sheriff will see to it that the families of Ivor and the other men will be paid for their sacrifice," John told Vessey. "Will you make sure they're given a good funeral?"

The bailiff had nodded sadly, sorry to have sent the four men off to their doom, although pleased that the notorious criminals from York had been brought to bloody justice. He also promised to send a messenger to York, to let the authorities there know that William Wake, and Grimbald de Pendok, killers of the town guardsmen, had been brought to justice by John and Tuck.

After that, the two friends had travelled again to Pontefract, arriving there on the morning of Christmas Eve. It was still snowing so the roads were practically deserted as waggons could not travel and even the horses found it hard going.

The riders did not speak a great deal on the road, for, although they'd completed the mission Bishop Wulstan had given them, the death of the men from Leeds weighed heavily on their shoulders.

"Let's just deliver the relic to All Saints'," John said gloomily as they rode into Pontefract. "And go home."

Tuck did not argue, did not even suggest stopping at the bakers even though it was located right across from their destination and they'd not enjoyed a proper hot meal in some time.

The church doors were closed when they reached it, and no wonder, given the frigid conditions. They opened when John lifted the latch though, and the men went inside gladly, cheered to be out of the biting gale for a time. The skin on the bailiff's face was chapped and raw after being blasted continually by that icy wind for days on end so it was a relief to be inside sturdy stone walls, even if there was no welcoming fire within All Saints'.

"It's good to see the place has been tidied after Tanner and his men's visit," Tuck said, examining the church interior.

"Aye, and now we can restore it properly with this," John agreed, reaching into his pack and removing the little wooden statuette that was held in such esteem, and worth so much that men had died for it.

The door leading to the vestry opened then, and they turned to see Bishop Wulstan.

"Ah! I heard someone talking and prayed to God it would be you. Where have you been? It's been days since you left! Did you—" He broke off as he noticed what John held in his hand and came to them, running, eyes shining in pure joy. "You brought it back! God be praised, it's a miracle."

"I wouldn't quite go that far, Your Grace," Tuck said, flushing in embarrassment.

"It is," Wulstan replied gleefully. "You see, the sick child is here. The family arrived yesterday but there's been no improvement in her condition." He lowered his voice and leaned in. "She's dying, I'm afraid. But now we have hope! Come!"

He spun on his heel and hurried towards the doors John and Tuck had entered through. They followed him, glancing at one another, neither relishing the thought of meeting a dying child. Still, they'd been commanded to follow, and they did so, walking behind the bishop as he led the way to the priest's house which was set just a little way off to the side of the church.

It was a small dwelling, but well-made and maintained. Someone had even hung garlands of ivy over the windows and door, and the smoke rising from the chimney hole at least promised the place would be warm. A robin landed on the thatched roof, head tilted, watching as they approached, its red breast adding another pleasant touch of colour to the scene.

Bishop Wulstan turned to them as they reached the house and opened his mouth as if about to say something, but he changed his mind, gave them both a serious look, and opened the door, dipping his head and ushering them inside.

John idly fiddled with his hood which he'd removed when they entered the church, and Tuck bowed and smiled to the people within the priest's little house. Father le Page was there, of course, and a man and a woman, both thin and pale, eyes red-rimmed and sunken. There was one, narrow bed in this room of the house and in it was a girl with chestnut brown hair, shivering despite the fact her face was damp with sweat. John wondered if he should even be in the house – what if her malady was catching? He pushed the thought aside, shamed by his lack of courage and empathy.

"This is John Little, and Friar Tuck," said the bishop, a triumphant tone in his voice that John found strange. They might have brought the relic back to Pontefract, but it hadn't done anything yet, and most likely never would. From the look of the poor child she was extremely unwell, and it would genuinely take a miracle to make her better. "They have retrieved the Virgin of the Mountains!"

Father le Page beamed as Bishop Wulstan brought the statuette out from beneath his cloak, and the parents of the child gasped, a wild hope flaring in their eyes that made Little John's heart ache. He had one child, a boy also called John – a man now in fact, and a forester at that. The thought of going through what these parents were suffering, watching their beloved daughter waste away day by day, hour by hour, was simply unimaginable.

"Did you hear that, Emily?" the woman asked in a cracked voice, reaching out and taking the girl's emaciated hand in hers. "The holy relic has been returned by these two men. Perhaps now you will get better."

"We shall pray," Bishop Wulstan said decisively, as though there was not a moment to spare. John guessed that might well be the case and bowed his head as the prayer began. He had expected it to be a far grander affair, with special candles lit, hymns sung, even a mass celebrated, but there was none of that, just a few simple prayers that everyone except the girl joined in with.

When they were finished there was no flash of lightning, no sudden appearance of the sun outside to lighten the lowering sky, no blast of heavenly trumpets, nothing. John lifted his eyes and glanced at Emily. She seemed to be asleep, sunken features appearing grey in the light of the fire. A lump formed in the bailiff's throat, and he knew their quest had been for naught.

There was no miracle.

Tuck went to the parents and blessed them softly, smiling encouragement before he followed the bishop back out into the cold. John could only manage a nod to the man and woman before he too left the priest's house, drawing in a long, frigid breath like a drowning man breaking the surface of the sea.

"Thank you both," Wulstan gushed, still apparently overjoyed despite the failure of the relic to heal Emily. "You will be staying the night here in Pontefract, I assume?"

John shook his head. "No. We want to be back home in Wakefield for Christmas Day."

"No chance of that now," Tuck said as the snow began once more, fat, heavy flakes falling as though sent to torment John who wanted nothing more than to see his wife, Amber, and put this whole sorry affair behind him.

"There is an inn just along the road there," said the bishop.

"Aye, Your Grace, that's where our horses are stabled," Tuck told him.

"Ah, very good. The proprietor knows me well – the church does a lot of business with him. You will find his establishment to be one of the better ones in Yorkshire, and, fear not, I will pay for your food and lodging. Come to see me before you leave on the morrow, eh?"

John felt a great sense of sadness, as if the falling white flakes carried some melancholy within them that seeped into his bones as he stood there, thinking of the men from Leeds who had died to bring back the useless relic. He wondered if Andrew, or any Apostle, had ever even seen the damned thing. Probably not.

"Thank you, Your Grace," Tuck was saying and the bishop, oblivious to John's mood, strode back to All Saints' to replace the Virgin of the Mountains in its rightful position.

Tuck looked up at his friend and must have guessed the reason for John's silence. "Come on," he said. "It's Christmas Eve. We might as well enjoy whatever entertainments the inn has to offer on such an auspicious day."

* * *

Little John awoke the next morning to the sound of bells. He and Tuck were in the same room, huddled in the same bed for warmth for, although this inn was larger than many, it did not have enough rooms for each patron to enjoy one of their own. Thankfully, they'd not been forced to share the bed with strangers, as was so often the case in establishments like that.

"It's past dawn already," the bailiff said, rising and washing his face in the bowl of water a servant had left out for them. Towelling himself dry he opened the shutter and peered out of the window, shivering as an icy blast of wind blew in.

"God's teeth, shut the window, man," Tuck cursed, rolling out of the bed and hastily throwing his cloak around his shoulders before washing his face. "Is it still snowing?"

John smiled. "No. We should be able to travel."

Tuck nodded. "Good, we'll be back in Wakefield by midday then. Come, let's break our fast and get on the road. It feels like the past couple of weeks have lasted forever and home is crying out to me."

"Amen," John murmured, fastening his own cloak around his massive shoulders and following the friar into the common room of the tavern.

The workers had been up through the night preparing fresh bread and a batch of ale for the customers, and both John and Tuck eagerly partook of both.

"Merry Christmas," Tuck said as he chewed bread and popped a piece of crumbly cheese into his mouth.

John grunted a noncommittal reply, still upset that their mission had resulted only in death. It did not seem right to him, especially on such a holy day. He expected his mood would improve once he was back in Wakefield with Amber, and dour Will Scaflock came to wish them the season's greetings in his own inimitable manner but, for now, he could not muster any enthusiasm.

"Cheer up, old friend," Tuck said. "We always knew the relic might not help the child."

John sighed heavily and continued to chew his bread without tasting it for a long moment. "I know," he said at last. "And we've seen enough death in our lives that we should be used to it. I just…"

"You thought there would be a Christmas miracle."

"Our efforts deserved it!" John nodded.

Tuck touched the cross around his neck and said, simply, "We do not always get what we deserve in this life. You know that better than anyone, John."

The friar's face was kindly, but John took his words as a rebuke and he finished the bread, trying to lighten his mood, reminding himself he would be with his own beloved family within just a couple of hours, if the roads were not too thick with snow and ice.

"We should visit All Saints' before we leave," Tuck said as they thanked the tavern keeper and headed out to collect their horses. "Bishop Wulstan told us to."

John let out a long breath. He really did not wish to set foot in the church again.

"Come on," called Tuck, already striding through the snow towards All Saints'. "We won't tarry long, but the bishop has been good to us in the past and it's always good to maintain cordial relations with powerful men like him."

Dawn Mass, heralded by the bells that had woken John, was over and the congregation streamed past the bailiff and the friar, all smiles and laughter as they looked forward to a day of feasting and pleasure. The church was quiet when

Tuck pulled open the door and went inside, eyes slowly growing accustomed to the gloom. The heady scent of incense hung heavy in the cool air and John breathed it in as he closed the door behind him.

"Bishop Wulstan must be in the vestry," Tuck said softly, not waiting to see if John would follow him. As they walked, an unexpected sound came to them and they pulled up, eyeing one another in confusion.

"Sounds like crying," John noted.

Friar Tuck nodded slowly. "A woman. Wait, a man too."

"Oh, God, it must be the child's parents." John held out a hand as though to push Tuck away and backed towards the doors. "Come on, let's get out of here. We can't intrude on their grief. The bishop will just have to wait to see us again."

"Hold!" The friar's tone was commanding and John paused. "Listen."

The bailiff stood in the empty church and listened. The sobs of a man and a woman were clear, but he noticed now that they were interspersed with another sound.

"They're laughing," said Tuck, a broad grin filling his round face. He did not hesitate, hurrying towards the rear of the church before knocking on the vestry door and letting himself in.

John came at his back, curiosity overcoming his trepidation and fear at what they might find within the chamber.

Bishop Wulstan was there, and he beamed to see them, hurrying across and embracing them both unashamedly. He was wearing the robes he had celebrated the dawn Mass in, and he threw out his arm, gesturing to the corner.

John saw now the parents of little Emily, and there too was the girl, no longer bedridden, her skin no longer the grey pallor of one close to death.

"You're better?" the giant asked, stepping slowly, almost cautiously, further into the chamber and staring down in amazement at the girl who stood shyly peering up at him. "Truly, you're better?"

"I think so," she said. Her eyes were wide but bore little trace of the red rings that had blighted them just the day before. "Merry Christmas, sir."

"Oh, Merry Christmas to you too, Emily!" John replied joyously. "Merry Christmas indeed, lass!"

EPILOGUE

The ride home from Pontefract to Wakefield was surprisingly pleasant in spite of the weather, and the miles passed quickly. The wind did not let up, biting the skin on John and Tuck's faces so they weren't sure if it was freezing or burning, and it began to snow yet again about a mile from the village as well.

"Typical," the bailiff said, looking up at the sky and grinning as he wiped damp flakes from his hood.

"Aye, it always starts just as we reach home," Tuck agreed with a laugh. "But we'll soon be in the alehouse, warm and dry, and enjoying plenty of Christmas cheer."

"And we'll not need to put our hands in our coin purses all night. The tale we've got to tell everyone will see us in drinks for a long time!"

They were spotted before they reached Wakefield, for children were playing in the snow on the outskirts of the village, faces red, smiles as wide as the River Calder. The youngsters knew John and Tuck by sight, and they ran to the men, calling out to ask where they'd been and what adventures they'd enjoyed this Yuletide.

"I'm going home to Amber," John said to the friar once they'd left the excited boys and girls behind. "She'll be worried about me."

"All right," Tuck nodded. "Then I'll ride on to the church. I'll meet you there for afternoon Mass."

John's face fell for he could not really be bothered standing in the draughty church while

Father Myrc sermonised. But then he remembered the miracle that had happened back in Pontefract and knew God should be thanked for His mercy. The bailiff smiled as he waved to Tuck, promising to be there when the bells rang out across the snow-covered land.

Amber had indeed been worried for her husband's safety, and let him know in no uncertain terms how unhappy she was when he arrived at their house.

"This is the first time in years that I haven't woken up beside you on Christmas morning," she scolded. "You better have a damn good excuse for being absent. I thought you'd been killed!"

John looked at her and thanked God for his own good fortune. She was in her mid-thirties like him, but she was far from grizzled as he was, with her pale, smooth skin and finely combed hair. He kissed her and she returned it, laughing breathlessly when he released her at last.

"I have a good excuse," he told her. "And you'll hear all about it soon enough. First let me change into some more suitable, and cleaner, clothes and we'll go celebrate with Tuck and whoever else is at afternoon Mass."

As always, All Hallows Church had been decorated for the season, with holly and ivy brightening the otherwise drab winter colours of the building, and the trees outside had been traditionally decorated with apples and communion wafers. Inside, Father Myrc had, for the first time, set up a model stable with a wooden manger, donkey, ox, and baby Jesus, all made by a local craftsman. The models were quite crudely carved and painted, but it was clear what they represented, and the priest gave a stirring Christmas sermon to the gathered villagers beside the little Nativity diorama before blessing everyone and sending them on their way to enjoy the festivities.

"I thought Father Myrc might have asked us to tell the tale of our adventures there in the church," John said as he, Amber, and Tuck made their way to the alehouse for a well-earned drink.

"He would have," the friar said, smiling in greeting to an elderly couple as they passed. "But I told him we'd been riding hard for days and were looking forward to putting our feet up."

"Holding court in the alehouse more like," Amber snorted, giving him a sidelong glance that made both men laugh.

"You know us too well, lady," Tuck conceded. "We have a fine story to tell, and All Hallows is far too cold for it. Look, here we are, and this is a more suitable venue for people to hear of our adventures."

They'd reached the alehouse and John pushed the door open, all three revelling in the warmth that spilled out from the hearth, and the noise from the patrons already gathered within to make the most of the holiday.

They were noticed immediately by the proprietor, Alexander Gilbert, who nodded in reply to John's vague hand signals. Somehow Alexander was always able to read those gestures perfectly so the bailiff knew three drinks and three warm meals would soon be brought out for them.

"Here! You two bastards!"

John flinched back as a meaty hand appeared from beside them, reaching for his collar. The bailiff had moved just in time, but the attacker simply grasped Tuck's cloak instead and shook the friar roughly.

"Where have you two been? Poor Amber was worried sick!"

"I think you were more worried than I was, Will," Amber laughed, slapping Scaflock's hand away from Tuck's shoulder. "You were almost in tears when I saw you this morning, wondering where your friends were."

"I was not!" Will retorted, before his angry expression became a broad grin and he laughed loudly. "Well, maybe I was a little bit worried about them. Where have you been you pair of arseholes? I thought you must be dead."

"As charming as ever," Tuck muttered, theatrically dusting himself off and heading for the nearest available table by the fire. "Come on, Will, you can pay Alexander for our drinks, and we'll tell you all about it."

As expected, once John and Tuck started regaling the patrons with the story of their recent adventures the drinks flowed and not once did either man have to spend a penny of their own. Alexander brought trenchers of roast duck, beef, and bacon and, when the story was finished, more people – including Will Scaflock's wife and little boy – had come into the alehouse and demanded they be told the whole tale from the beginning. In between eating, drinking, and acting out the most exciting or dramatic parts of the tale the villagers gathered around the fire and sang carols. Even

Father Myrc came in as night fell and led them all in a rousing rendition of *"In Dulci Jubilo",* the higher voices of the women and children harmonising sweetly with the lower registers of the men.

In all, it was a fine way to round out an unexpectedly intense and difficult few days for Little John and Friar Tuck, and both men were in good spirits as dice were brought out and folk crowded around to enjoy the games, some even draping garlands of ivy around their friends and partner's shoulders and heads.

"I'm just nipping out to the privy," Little John said to Amber who looked up at him from shining eyes. "I won't be long," he said, chuckling to himself for no apparent reason as he went to the door and hauled it open. He steadied himself for a moment before the angry shouts of the other patrons chased him outside and he banged the door shut behind him against the wind and the swirling snow.

The privy was located at the rear of the tavern and consisted of little more than a wooden shelter with some buckets to collect waste. It was dark, but John knew from long experience which side the tavern's buckets for piss were on and he fumbled with his breeches before relieving himself with a sigh. Behind him he could hear the happy chatter and laughter of his friends and neighbours, and he thought again of the holy relic that had healed the child.

He and Tuck had done a good thing that Christmas, and he wasn't ashamed to admit it felt good to know he'd helped that family.

The wind rattled the rickety old roof over the privy and John hastily sorted his breeches before heading back towards the tavern, taking a long, deep breath of the cold night air.

"Hello, John."

The bailiff's pleasant feeling of drunkenness instantly evaporated and his hand fell to the knife he always carried in a sheath at his waist. His shambling gait transformed into a towering, defensive stance and he demanded, "Who's that?" for the voice seemed familiar, yet he could not quite place it.

"It's me," said a man, and John turned to look into the shadows cast by the alehouse wall. "Hal Tanner."

"Tanner! What the hell are you doing here, lurking about privies on Christmas Day in the dark?"

There was silence for a long moment and then, at last, Tanner said almost apologetically. "I just wondered if you knew what had happened to the sickly child you said the Virgin of the Mountains was supposed to help. Did she, well, did the relic do anything?"

John grinned, teeth showing white in the snowy gloom. "It did," he said. "It was a miracle, Tanner, you should have been there. We took the relic back yesterday and nothing seemed to happen, but this morning, when we went to All Saints', the girl – Emily – was all better. It was truly a miracle!"

"A miracle," Tanner's voice was low, but John could see the outlaw's expression had transformed into a smile.

"Letting us take that relic was the right thing to do," John said, nodding. "You did your part in saving the girl, Tanner. Thank you."

"You don't have to thank me. But..." He trailed off and his head dipped as he searched in his pack for something. "Here. Would you see that the girl's family gets this? You said they were poor. Maybe this will help her family, and the lass won't get sick again if they can afford decent food and warm clothes for her."

John took the proffered bag and knew immediately that it was filled with coins.

"Must be a good few pounds in here," the bailiff said without looking into the bag. "You sure you won't need it yourself? Life as an outlaw is not easy, Hal, trust me."

Tanner nodded again. "The girl's family needs it more than I do. Like you, I've done some bad deeds in my life, John. Maybe this will go some way to putting things right. It's a start at least." He chuckled without mirth. "Ask your mate the friar to say a few prayers for my soul this Christmas Night, eh? Can't hurt."

"I will. Where shall you go now though?" John jerked his chin towards the rowdy tavern, an oasis of life and laughter in the frozen Yorkshire night. "You're more than welcome to join us for a drink and a game of dice."

Tanner shook his head. "I'm heading to Skipton."

"Skipton? What's there?"

Tanner let out a wistful sigh.

"Someone I haven't seen in a long while," he said, shaking his head. "Maybe it's been too long."

He shrugged and gave a thin smile. "Or perhaps there'll be another Christmas miracle. Whatever happens, I still have a few coins in my pack. I'll be all right." He thrust out his forearm and the bailiff grasped it firmly. "Look after yourself, John."

John was intrigued by Tanner's words, but could see the man was done talking.

"You too, Hal. You too."

Tanner gave a sombre salute and walked towards the road where, John now realised, a horse stood, waiting patiently for its master's return. The outlaw mounted the animal nimbly and turned back one last time, hand raised in the falling snow in farewell.

"Hey, Tanner!" John called as the horse trotted into the darkness, the snow swirling about him.

"Aye?"

"Merry Christmas!"

There was a pause. Tanner did not turn in the saddle, but his voice came from the gloom.

"And a merry Christmas to you too, John Little. Merry Christmas, one and all!"

THE END

AUTHORS' NOTES

STEVEN A. McKAY

As many of you will know, I co-hosted a podcast called Rock, Paper, Swords with Matthew for three years. I've since stepped down and been replaced by the brilliant Justin Hill, but in the time I was doing it we sometimes spoke about how authors collaborated together on novels. Did the authors write a chapter each? Did one person have most of the ideas and do most of the work with the other coming in and adding colour to it? How were royalties split? How well could a collaboration even work? Wouldn't the different styles dilute the overall story? And who gets their name first on the cover?!

I don't actually remember how we decided that we should find out the answers to all these questions by writing a book of our own together, but that's what happened and *Swords in the Snow* is the result. Each writing 'team' will have a different way of working I'm sure, but for this novella we thought taking a chapter each would be the simplest way to do things. It didn't turn out like that once we got started though, as the story just didn't flow as neatly as that (it would have been a very stilted tale if we'd stuck rigidly to it). Instead, we both took short sections of the story and wrote each to its natural conclusion – this meant that I was given the task of starting AND ending it all, even though Matthew was the first to sit down and write anything for it! At first it felt like I was just setting things up for Matthew to then come in and write all the fun, action-packed sections, but it began to even out as things got going and we both thoroughly enjoyed what we were coming up with.

Of course, we had a basic framework for the setting, since the characters and 'world' are taken from my Forest Lord stories which I always publish around Christmastime. That gave me a familiar foundation, but it meant Matthew had to invent some new characters like Wake and Tanner and then slot them into the setting I'd been building for the past 12 years since *Wolf's Head* came out. I have to say, I think Matthew did an admirable job, not just in coming up with memorable characters, but in keeping his own style while somehow fitting neatly into the Forest Lord setting. When I read his parts combined with my own I genuinely believed readers would thoroughly enjoy what we'd written.

It took us most of 2025 to write the book, simply because we were working on it in between other, full-length novels. It was always fun to come back to *Swords in the Snow* though, and we had lots of detailed chats about where things should go next, what character should do what, which relic we should include, how to solve issues that arose as we went along. You can listen to those chats, as we recorded them and put them out as podcast episodes on the Rock, Paper, Swords Patreon. If you haven't heard them yet, you should check them out as they provide an interesting 'diary' charting our progress pretty much from beginning to end. I don't know if anyone has ever done anything like that before, but it really does give an insight into how a collaboration like this can be done.

For me, I found it very refreshing to pit my beloved characters, Tuck and John, against a villain *that I had not created*. It almost made things more organic, more interesting, because I genuinely had no idea what Tanner and Grimbald and the rest would get up to in each chapter. Don't get me wrong, I know this isn't the most intricately plotted work of fiction, but I think the combination of writing styles and ideas gives the book an added dimension.

As I said before, I've been writing Christmas/winter novellas for a few years now – I just love this snowy season, and I know many of my readers do too. Lots of you look forward to my Xmas tales so I hope you found *Swords in the Snow* a worthy addition to the collection. Going forward, now that Robin has come back into the fold in *Return of the Wolf,* maybe he will join Tuck, John, and Will Scaflock for future frostbitten novellas, I've not decided yet. Join me to find out!

Thank you for reading, everyone. Have a fantastic Christmas, and here's to a brilliant 2026 for us all!

Steven A. McKay
Old Kilpatrick
4th September 2025

MATTHEW HARFFY

Like Steven, I can't recall the exact moment we came up with the idea of writing a novella together, but I think it must have been shortly after we spent a few days together at the Historical Novel Society Conference in Devon in September 2024.

We had a great time at the event, which we attended as the official podcasters, and in many ways it marked the zenith of our collaboration on the podcast, with a whole weekend living and breathing historical fiction, meeting countless authors, and even getting to interview giants of the genre like the lovely Diana Gabaldon, and our literary hero, Bernard Cornwell.

It was at the HNS 2024 conference that we met and interviewed A. D. Rhine (the pseudonym of the writing team made up of old school friends, Ashlee Cowles and Danielle Stinson). Our conversation with Ashlee and Danielle left Steven and I intrigued by the process of collaborative writing, and, as Steven puts out a novella around Christmas every year, and there was no way we were going to find the time to write a whole novel, working together on a winter novella set in the world of The Forest Lord series, made perfect sense.

Our schedules also aligned, with me having a few weeks between novels at the start of 2025, where I could write the bulk of my sections, with Steven picking it up and adding his parts later in the summer when one of his novels was off to the editor.

It worked out really well, I think. I thoroughly enjoyed throwing myself into the world of the 14th century and creating some new characters to act as foils for Steven's wonderful heroes. From the beginning, we knew we didn't just want me to create moustache-twirling villains, and so I came up with Henry (Hal) Tanner, a tough man in a dark world, someone willing to steal and kill, but with some redeeming qualities. Around him, the characters of William Wake, Grimbald de Pendok, Richard Blount and the others just fell into place, and once I started writing, the words flowed.

The most challenging moments came later after Steven had written his own sections and we had to make sure that all of the timelines and motivations aligned. This is where you realise that, however much we had discussed and planned the structure of the story, and it was a simple story at that, so much of the process of writing is held in the author's head. Tiny decisions are taken without forethought and then forgotten, and it was only when Steven read through it and asked me about some of those decisions that I was forced to question myself.

This is traditionally the work of the editor, and I think both Steven and I found value in being edited by each other. I knew my characters better than Steven, but this is his world, and Little John and Friar Tuck have had countless adventures together over the years. Steven knows them intimately and I found it quite amusing that he was a bit put out on behalf of Little John that I had created Grimbald, who might even be bigger than the bailiff! I think some of John Little's annoyance at the comparison between the two of them was actually Steven voicing his own umbrage!

A quick note on the choice of the relic in the story. In January 2025, I visited a friend of mine in Spain and we stayed in Sotosalbos, a small village north of Madrid. While there, we went inside the village's picturesque 12th century Romanesque church, Iglesia de San Miguel Arcangel (Church of Saint Michael Archangel), and, within the vestry, I saw a simply painted wooden figure of the Virgin Mary holding the baby Jesus. It was dated as from the 12th century and named, "Virgen de la Sierra" (Virgin of the Mountains). We had found our relic.

For the "miraculous" cure of the child, we needed an illness that could appear fatal, but from which the child would then spontaneously recover. We settled on typhus, the symptoms of which are high fever, delirium, a rash, and sometimes a coma-like state. The fever can break suddenly after twelve to fourteen days, and a patient can go from near-death to recovering overnight.

This fit the narrative perfectly and, of course, the characters (and readers!) can make up their own mind as to whether God intervened in this Christmas miracle.

Merry Christmas, and I hope you enjoy this tale as much as Steven and I enjoyed writing it.

Matthew Harffy
Wiltshire
8th September 2025

ACKNOWLEDGEMENTS

Thanks to our beta readers, and the Rock, Paper, Swords Patreon Producers, Gareth Jones, Bernadette McDade, Adam Turner, Ben Maher, Andy Maxwell, Ben Fox, Daryl Haire and George Johnson.

Printed in Dunstable, United Kingdom